Printed in the United States of America
First Printing, 2021
ISBN 978-1-7349192-5-7 (paperback)
978-1-7349192-4-0 (ebook)

TALES OF
ELHAANAI
BOOK TWO

THE PROPHECY

Dedication

To the readers who became a writer.
To the writers who never stopped reading.
To the dreamers and the doers.
To the ones waiting to begin.

INDEX

ELHAANAI

Wastelands
Utata Manor
Vimeo
Arcana
Damu Manor
Mnara Mountains
Oasis
Dire den
Ashreks tunnel
Nuru Manor
Egan
Farm
Spyre River
Forbidden Wood
elhasheda
elphanuel
ELHAANAI

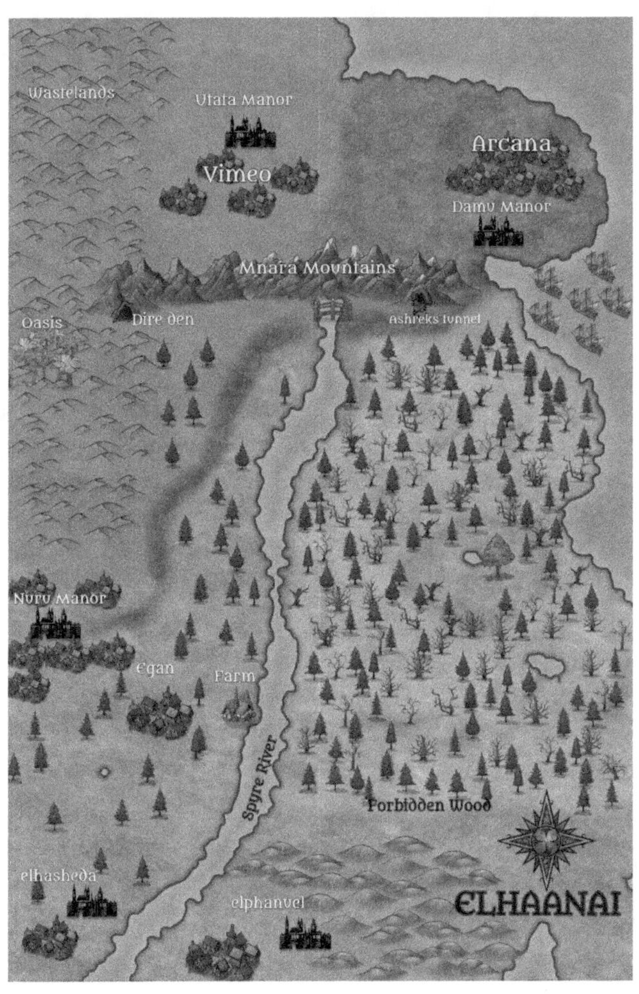

Chapter 1

"YOUR MAJESTY!" The captain of the guard put one foot back and bowed from the waist.

"Akronius, this isn't exactly the time to show your allegiance to…" Alric suddenly realized Akronius wasn't addressing him. He was bowing to the man in chains, who sat with his back against the dungeon wall.

"It can't be," choked Alric with widened eyes.

"Yes, it can, and it is. Alric, this man is King Kaison, your father."

"My what? You don't look dead!"

"How observant of you. No, I am not. Although, I have certainly wished for death many times over the last few years. I am grateful that The One chose to ignore that particular request." Kaison grew quiet and stared at Alric for several moments; "I can see so much of your mother in your face."

Turning to Akronius he continued, "I can only assume the explanation behind you and my son traveling together is a long one. Can we leave this place so we can get better acquainted in a more conducive setting, before Chumbra returns and foils your rescue?"

"Of course, Your Majesty. Follow me! Alric, let's go."

Kaison held up his wrists and shook them slightly. "Forgetting something?"

"Oh right." Alric looked at Akronius. "Can any of your new senses break chains?"

"Why don't you try channeling through your bond with Elainea? Her fire should melt the bolt in the wall, and she can figure out the rest back at the farm."

Alric closed his eyes and focused on his sister like Shama had trained him to do. He felt their connection and then followed the heat to its source, pulling it to the forefront of his mind. Eyes still closed, he placed his palm on the bolt that was securing his father's chains to the wall. It dropped from the hole like molten rock.

Alric opened his eyes and found his father staring at him in awe.

"You are very strong. Fire? What else are you gifted with?"

Alric wiped the sweat from his face. "Well, it's not my gift exactly. It's Elainea's, my sister, but I can sort of borrow it."

"Sister? What do you mean?" Kaison steadied himself on the stone wall as he stood, his legs trembling beneath him.

"It's a long story. Let's get you out of here first."

Akronius went to assist the King as he moved toward the wooden door only to be met with a scowl. He backed away allowing Alric to take his place as they headed for the stairs. The trio moved slowly. Akronius' eyes showed an amber glow as he tuned his senses to their surroundings.

"We have to hurry. Men are coming from the main road."

Kaison looked at Akronius and stumbled, "How do you know that? Your eyes! Since when are you gifted?"

"It's a long story Your Majesty." Akronius sighed, "I promise we will answer all your questions as soon as we are safe."

The men hurried as quickly as they could; back up the stairs to the crypt, still avoiding the green luminescent plant life.

King Kaison slowed for a moment as they passed a sarcophagus with his name on it. "So, this is where I was buried. I had no idea where I was all this time. Somehow fitting, I suppose." Traveling back through the darkness as silently as they had come, they paused at the rusted gate. Akronius began to whistle softly, a series of short chirps and clicks. A responsive call came from the thick canopy of trees nearby followed by another a little farther away.

"There are five men riding this way, if we hurry, we can get around them without being detected. Follow me."

"If I had not witnessed it with my own eyes and ears, I would not have believed it. How could The One bestow on you such a gift? The very same gift that was taken from me!" Enraged, the veins in Kaison's clenched hands were clearly visible through his parchment thin skin.

Alric looked between the two men, who could not have been that far apart in age, and sighed. He understood his father's anger, but he knew they did not have the time for it at that moment. Stepping between them he placed a steadying hand on his father's shoulder, which forced eye contact to shift his way.

"Your Majesty... Father, please. We will explain everything soon, I promise, but please, I trust him with my life; so, trust me."

Kaison glanced down and gave a faint nod, though his jaw was clenched so tightly it looked as if it would break.

Just then, an alarm sounded behind them coming from Nuru Manor. The place had once been a happy home, now it was no more than a fortified enclosure. Trumpets blasted, dogs barked and that was all they needed to hasten their pace.

Chapter 2

FOR DAYS, FATHER AND SON followed silently behind Akronius, who stopped every so often to receive instructions from his winged scouts. They moved within the shadows of large trees, stepping over roots and broken branches. When they were far enough away, Akronius reached into his pack and withdrew a small pouch. From this, he took a handful of seeds and dropped them in a pile. Three Chatterie birds swooped down from the branches. One landed on Akronius' shoulder and nuzzled his cheek, as if in appreciation for the food. As they flew away, Akronius once again met the smoldering gaze of Kaison, neither man willing to look away.

Clearing his throat, Alric nudged Akronius forward, breaking the growing tension so they could keep moving to reach the farm and rest.

Nothing was said as they traveled through the woods, skirting towns and avoiding as many people as possible. Akronius held up a hand to pause their forward movement when they came too close to someone passing and simply moved onward when it was all clear, they followed obediently. When the farm was in sight, Akronius indicated they should stay in the shadows of the tree line while he went ahead to make sure it was safe to bring the king in. They had no way of knowing if their location had been discovered during their time away, they could be walking into a trap. Akronius crept through the yard, careful to avoid tools strewn about as he made his way to the window that was illuminated by a single candle. Seeing only Elainea with her hands clasped before her, lips moving silently, he moved to the door and entered slowly.

"Akronius! You're back!" She rushed to him in relief, and then glanced behind him into the darkness. "But why are you alone? Where is my brother? I will murder you in your sleep if he has been caught! I will boil your brains within your skull! I will…" Magic brimmed in her fingers, sparks fluttered from the tips like tiny arrows as her hair moved on the current of heat rising from her.

"Calm down Elainea, he is fine." Akronius said firmly, casting a glance at the glow pulsating from her hands. "He is waiting at the tree line with a guest. I had to make sure no soldiers had come here before bringing him in."

"Oh, I'm sorry. I didn't really mean those things you know." She let the sentence fall off without finishing because they both knew she would do all those things, and more, if any harm had come to her brother. Clearing her throat and straightening her dress she asked, "Who is the guest?"

"You wouldn't believe me if I told you." He stood in the doorway and let a shrill whistle out. Two shadows emerged from the darkness of the trees and made their way toward the farmhouse. Stepping inside the doorway Alric was immediately enveloped by his sister.

"Alric, I'm so glad you're safe!" She hugged him tightly. "Did you find the answers you were looking for?"

"Actually, no, only more questions. Elainea, this is King Kaison, my father."

"Is this really the best time for a joke? The King died ages ago. Who is this man?" She looked from one face to the other, before settling on the man claiming to be Alric's father.

"Trust me I am just as shocked as you are, young lady."

"My name is Elainea. Your Majesty?" She was not certain what she should call him and looked to her brother for direction.

"Yes, he is the king or he will be again, I suppose. I don't know. There is a lot we need to discuss."

"Yes, there is," Kaison said while lifting his still shackled wrists. "But first things first. Elainea, can you remove the rest of these chains from my wrists please? And then, I hope you have plenty of food, for I am starving."

"Ha! Maybe he really is your father!" She reached for his shackles and uttered a quick spell that unlocked them. He rubbed his wrists as the chains fell to the floor. Raising a hand to indicate a pot hanging over the dying embers of a fire, "I have a light meal prepared. Naia brought down a small deer earlier today."

"Ah, my thanks to Naia! Where is she?" Kaison looked around the small home.

"She is under the table, Sir." Elainea said blushing.

"Under the... what?"

Kaison bent over and glanced under the table, "Oh a wolf! Of course. Thank you Naia."

"She says you are welcome." Akronius translated the yips for those present. He left out her saying, *'not to get used to it as food was for pack mates only, of which he is not.'*

Kaison did not even acknowledge that Akronius had spoken; instead he kept his back to the other man, focusing on Alric and then turning to Elainea as she handed him a bowl of stew.

"Thank you, my dear daughter." Kaison sat at the table and began devouring the food in the same way Alric did, barely a breath between bites as if it were his last meal.

"You are welcome, but I am not your daughter." Elainea looked between Alric and Akronius, her brows drawn together in confusion. "Did they not explain this to you?"

"No, we did not have the time. There were guards around and we were more concerned with our safety than explanations at the time. Once we have all eaten, we can talk." Akronius almost growled as he walked over to fill his own bowl with stew. His patience was growing short at being ignored by Kaison. King or not, the man would still be rotting away in a crypt if he hadn't taken Alric there to pay respects to the supposedly dead man. He'd still be a slave to that black-magic-wielding Chumbra, and subject to all the Oracle's experiments.

"Alric! My Boy! Come let me look at you." Alric sat in the chair across from Kaison, timidly looking into the face of his father. "I cannot tell you how many nights I sat in that cell and wondered if you had survived. And if you did, what you would look like. Who had you become. Your mother and I had such high hopes for you, such great expectations."

Kaison glanced down into his now empty bowl. His countenance darkened as he clenched and unclenched his fingers around the roughly carved wooden spoon. The grief was almost palpable beneath the weight of his next question.

"Tell me, did she survive? Alanna, your mother?"

The silence stretched for what seemed like an eternity before Alric answered quietly.

"No. She did not."

"How?" One word spoken with such frailty and brokenness made every eye in the room water at the memory.

Akronius looked across the room and caught Alric's eye. Both thinking of the part Akronius had played in Alanna's death. His frustration disappeared along with his appetite as he nodded slightly to

Alric and left the home. This was a conversation for which he would not want to be present.

14

Chapter 3

CHUMBRA MADE HIS WAY BACK to the manor with his final ingredient safely in hand. He could begin the preparations for his master immediately. He noticed an increase in guard activity at each town he passed through and wondered what was going on. People hurried along the muddy, pot-holed roads, scurried into homes, quickly closing doors behind them. The grasslands surrounding the Manor were uncommonly empty; farm animals slaughtered to feed families instead of traded in the market; and the absence of those trading stalls left a gaping void and bleakness to what was once a thriving market.

As he neared the Manor wall, a harried guard rushed to him, wide-eyed and out of breath. "King David has requested your presence, immediately upon your return," he panted.

Chumbra nodded mutely and followed the unsteady man inside. Reaching the throne room the guard was visibly relieved to go on his way.

A gaunt, anxious looking man with a golden crown upon his head leaned forward on spying Chumbra crossing the room. "Chumbra! I am very glad to see you returned safely. I trust you had no trouble obtaining the last ingredient?" His voice rasped and his dark eyes darted around the room, never resting in one place for too long; bouncing from the Oracle's face to the windows, the doors, the secret doors and back again.

"Yes, Your Majesty. I have what I need. I noticed many more guards traveling the roads and in the towns on my way back. Has something happened?" Chumbra followed the sight lines of King David, inspecting the windows and then the secret passageway doors hidden in the shadows.

"Yes, Chumbra, something has happened. My allies have turned into enemies and my mother is dead. The bells have been rung, and the guards dispersed to seek out the enemy." King David's bottomless black eyes bore into Chumbra's.

"DEAD? Surely you are mistaken! Devona is a strong woman. The Dark Lord would protect her from harm. I am sure of it. Where did you get this misinformation?"

"I saw it with my own eyes! The spell you placed on the earrings allowed me to watch as Ashrek… somehow drained all the life from her. She withered away before me like a grape left in the sun. She was barely a husk and still she lived! Ashrek instructed me to say goodbye and crushed the jewelry before I could see the killing blow, but the fear in her eyes was evident. It was not an expression I have ever seen on her." The king's eyes seemed to grow darker and a vein pulsed slightly in his forehead as he retold the events. In the short time David had been poisoned with dark magic he'd become barely recognizable. His thick flowing locks were now gone. A wisp of his thin lackluster hair fell across his sweating brow, lying like a scar against his pasty skin.

"My King, I do not know what to say! I am sorry. I will look through my texts to find out what kind of gift this Ashrek must have to accomplish such brutality." Chumbra took a step backwards toward the door.

"Yes, do that! And how is the other task you were assigned coming along? Is the potion ready for me to take?"

"My Lord, I have just returned with the final ingredient, remember?" Chumbra looked at the King in confusion. "I came straight here at your behest. I will start both the research and the preparations immediately."

"See that you do. I can take no chances now that Ashrek has made his intentions clear. I MUST possess the most power, more than anyone else alive!" David answered, not acknowledging Chumbra's confusion at all.

"And you will. You will have the ability to absorb any gift you come in contact with, stripping it away from the bearer as if it were no more than a cloak, and then wield it yourself. You will be unstoppable!"

"Perfect. GO!"

Chumbra bowed and hurried from the King's chamber. He turned for a final glance at the King as he silently closed the door. David stood smiling before the mirror, inspecting his appearance. Something he had stopped doing long ago. Mirrors had been forbidden; it was clear that whatever image was reflected back at the king now was not an accurate representation of reality. Chumbra could not be entirely sure, but it looked as if the king's reflection turned to meet his eye a moment before the king actually turned. Both the king and his reflection gave such a malevolent smile that it caused the hairs on the back of Chumbra's neck to stand on end as he finally closed the door. The potion would make the man powerful, but not in the way he thought. Smiling to himself, Chumbra was anxious to complete his task and finally open the path for his master to make his grand entrance.

Chapter 4

AKRONIUS SAT BY THE RIVER, with Naia at his feet, watching the final purple and pink streaks of daylight fade to the dark blue of night. He could feel the air tense around him and saw Naia turn her ears toward the approaching footsteps. Though he tried to calm himself, he felt his pulse and breath quicken with each step.

"What do the animals speak of tonight, Akronius?" Kaison said softly as he approached the river's edge.

Akronius closed his eyes and exhaled the breath he had been holding. He focused on the myriad of noises coming from their surroundings. He had learned to separate each sound in order to distinguish individuals, pushing the gurgling of the river as it flowed over the rocks and the wind gently creaking branches into the background, so that he was able to focus on the life around him.

"There are a few fish struggling to make their way upriver to warmer temperatures, two males who are worried they will miss out on all the strong eggs." Turning his head slightly he was able to hear more. "There is also a small hare nearby, trying to stay downwind of us and a... tic, I believe, complaining that Naia is not getting enough meat. Her blood is no longer as sweet as it used to be." He chuckled despite himself. He never grew tired of listening in on the strange conversations that went on all around them. He opened his eyes to see Kaison crouching at the river's edge, tossing stones in, watching the ripples.

"It is amazing to think we go about our day completely oblivious to the squabbles and constant conversations of the creatures we deem beneath us, how loud they can be. To hear you speak of it reminds me how much I miss the noise."

"How did you lose your gift, Your Majesty?" Akronius paused; he meant no disrespect but wanted to know.

"It is alright, you may call me Kaison. My time of ruling seems to be long past. Chumbra poisoned me when I went to breakfast that morning, as you well know. I woke up chained in that cell, extremely weak. I could still hear the surrounding animals, but I could not communicate with them. As time passed and Chumbra continued to drug me, I stopped hearing them altogether. It was as if a piece of my soul was removed, I could feel the void. He used me for my blood, to enhance his spells. I was powerless against him. I believe by keeping me in this weakened state, my gift has shriveled up. I am hoping, as my system purges itself, that it will return. Only The One knows."

The two men settled into an uncomfortable silence, both knowing what must be addressed, but neither wishing to breach that wall. Finally, it was Naia who broke the tension.

"Tell him, his bond with us is still there, though deep inside him. I can still see the faint glow of it. I can hear his words as if they were spoken from a great distance. Tell him, King Kaison is spoken of in our legends, we know of his fortitude. It will return in time."

Akronius relayed the message to Kaison whose back was still toward him. His shoulders dropped in relief. "Thank you, Naia. Thank you."

Silence once again settled between the two men, but it was no longer as strained as it was. Naia rose and stretched her body. She slowly approached Kaison and allowed him to scratch her head. She turned to leave brushing against Akronius, swatting him with her tail in the process.

"That means you are part of her pack. She leaves her scent on you and vice-a-versa. She considers you family. That is high praise from a dire wolf," said Kaison.

"Dire wolf?"

Kaison turned to Akronius in shock. "You have bonded with her but do not know what she is?"

"No, I mean... I did not bond with her. She was raised by Wleia, after her mother died. I thought dire wolves were larger."

"You have much to learn. She is young yet, and has quite a bit of growing to do. She likely is not a full-blooded dire wolf as the breed was hunted to near extinction for their pelts. A full-blooded male stood as tall as a grown man, fangs the length of my hand. They were a sight to behold. Do not worry Akronius, I will teach you about this gift we share."

Akronius looked Kaison in the eyes, unsure if he could believe what he was hearing. He knew of Kaison's strength as well, that he could channel the traits of countless animals. If he truly agreed to train him, he couldn't even fathom the depth of knowledge that would be available to him. But he had to know.

"Kaison… I am humbled you would offer this. But are you sure? After all you have been through; after everything you have learned; after my role in the… past?"

Kaison looked at Akronius and a flash of anger passed over his features, followed quickly by what looked like hate and regret, before settling somewhere in the middle, with a sigh.

"Alanna was the love of my life. She was my soul mate. Until you have one, if you are ever blessed enough to find that connection, you cannot know the pain caused by the loss of it. I do not know if I will ever forgive you. The One knows what I will do when my path crosses with Devona, but for now, I can work with the man you are today. I cannot change the past; it has shaped us all in irreversible ways. Alanna…," Akronius could see the struggle even mentioning her name caused Kaison. "Alanna's faith in The One was unshakable. She believed everyone was capable of change, change for the better or change for the worse. If I had only listened to her… ahh! Nothing to be done now, except move forward. So, yes, despite the fact that you contributed to the death of my wife, I will train you in order for us to place her son on the throne. We have a chance to return Elhaanai to the beautiful land it once was, the way The One intended it to be. We can only do that together."

Chapter 5

AS THE TWO MEN STARTED WALKING back toward the small house, Kaison asked, "Why have you not bonded with Naia?"

"According to Wleia, Naia is not mine to bond with. She alluded to the fact that I would have a different match. Naia is family, but will travel her own path when the time comes." Looking down he added, "I also do not know how the bonding process works. Did you ever have a bond?"

"Yes, I did. I was bonded to a falcon, Sheirra. She was my best friend for many years. Sadly, I do not know what became of her."

"How are bonds formed?"

"It is hard to explain. When you meet your familiar, something just clicks inside you. It's like a spark. Then you will have a constant connection to her. Men are paired with female animals and females with male animals. I believe this somehow deepens the bond."

"Considering that, I can understand why you would think Naia was my familiar. That would also rule out Auni."

"Auni?"

"He is a Firauni bird, I have become acquainted with."

"What? You have quite the menagerie around you Akronius. Those birds are very rare, and seldom allow humans to keep company with them. The One truly has his hand on you. I wonder what creature will bond with you. It will have to be an extremely noble one, considering the company you already keep."

"I wonder as well. Only time and The One will tell."

The home did not have enough rooms to accommodate them all, so, as Kaison entered, Akronius made his way to the barn. He would bunk with the four-legged and winged part of their group for the night. He let his eyes adjust to the darkness as he settled down into the hay. He was used to rough accommodations and the hay would keep him warmer than sleeping under the autumn sky. Above him Auni nested, one eye opened which watched him, silently.

'Is it true? King Kaison has returned?' Auni inquired.

'Yes, it is! Naia said he was spoken of in Animal Lore.'

'Yes, He was! He was the most powerful of familiars. His match is referenced by us in much the same way as Elrond is mentioned by mankind. If he has returned, then the prophecy is true... I will be gone for several days; I will return as soon as I am able.'

'What does the prophecy say?'

'It is not yet time for you to know. But I will tell you this, you will have a very important role in its fulfillment. Rest now, time is shifting like sand.'

Akronius considered the words of his friend. He wondered about the prophecy Auni had spoken of and what role he would come to play in it. As he drifted off to sleep, he felt a sharp pull in his chest. It created an ache he could not rub away. He fell asleep with the sound of flints being repeatedly struck against each other echoing in his mind.

Chapter 6

KING DAVID PACED FROM ONE END of his chambers to the other, his caramel colored hair stuck in all directions from his nervous hands running through it. His royal cloak was fraying in several spots as he pulled it around himself one moment and opened it the next. He pulled the sleeves up his arms to relieve the heat he felt and then instantly pulled them back down seeing the scars from his perfectly manicured nails as he absentmindedly scratched in his anxiety. The voice in his head had grown so loud that he could no longer tell the difference between it and his own thoughts. Chumbra had promised the potion he was creating would not only provide him with the means to become the most powerful man in the land, but would silence the voice as well. The voice told him to do things, unspeakable things. Some had proven wise, like the imprisonment of traitors, and the construction of new temples for foreigners to worship their Dark Lord, but it also asked for human sacrifices; to make them an example of what happened to traitors. He drew the line there. What Chumbra did with the prisoners was none of his concern, but he would not willingly order the death of his people. It was wrong. Right? Yes, right. No it was wrong.

Wrong? Who determines what is right or wrong, if not the King! You can do anything you want to do. The people will listen; they MUST listen to you or face the consequences. You do not want to be weak like your mother, do you? She tried to make you weak, to keep you weak. You are strong. Together we can be even stronger. Embrace the darkness David, like you did so long ago. Remember how good it felt? How RIGHT it felt. It's natural David. You are destined for greatness. EMBRACE THE DARKNESS. Your name will be repeated throughout all time. You will be worshiped. Revered. EMBRACE THE DARKNESS David. EMBRACE…. ME!

David squeezed his eyes shut but could feel his resolve slipping each day as the voice wore him down. He wanted to slip into the shadows, truly he did. To feel the power slip over his skin as he walked invisible among the people. To drown his own fear in theirs, to sink beneath the power of the darkness. To soak in the delicious fear of his subjects. His face began to relax at the thought, his body partially sinking into the shadows of his room.

'Yes, do it. Control it. You are strong enough.'

"NOOOO! BE SILENT!" David ripped himself from the shadow creeping up his body. "You do not control me, nor do you tell me what to do. I will be rid of you shortly. Be silent!" Looking wildly around, King David sank to a chair before his fireplace with his head in his hands. "Please, be silent. Be silent! Be silent! Be silent! Be silent!"

'NEVER!'

Chapter 7

ASHREK WALKED THE HALLS of his new manor, *his* manor! He liked the sound of that. No one missed Lord Vicrano, least of all him. He had spent years pandering to the man and his evil daughter, but no more. Arriving at the war room, he surveyed the maps strewn across the oak table. The tunnel was complete as was the main road around the mountains. His father had never arrived and Ashrek did not expect him to after receiving a letter that was both congratulatory and dismissive. Lord Overton was working on his own plans, as was his uncle Alcherist. The latter was not at all happy with the turn of events. He had wanted to take his own form of revenge, and felt Ashrek robbed him of that chance. Ashrek would have to watch him carefully, for the desire for revenge could overpower even the most loyal of blood lines.

A whine drew his gaze to the corner of the room where he had chained Vicrano's hounds. They were starving. He could count the bones protruding from their bodies. All the fight and resistance had drained from their eyes. He was their Master now, and he would break every person who stood in his way in the same manner.

"Hungry Boys? Let's go find something you can chew on." Ashrek took them from the room, down the hall, to a door in the back of the manor. Fitting his key in the lock, he pushed it open to reveal an emaciated Sybella. She lay in the middle of a large bed, beads of sweat on her forehead and greasy hair matted to the soiled pillow. A tear leaked from the corner of one eye.

"P-P-Please....w-w-w-a-a-t-t-e-e-r-r....p-p-p-l-ease." Her voice was scratchy and as cracked as her dry lips.

"What was that? Speak a little louder, Wife, I can hardly hear you." Ashrek walked further into the room with the dogs at his side. Stopping at the bedside table, he lifted the clear glass of water he had left there. Bringing it to his lips, he drank all but one mouthful.

"Do you want this Sybella? Are you willing to obey me completely?"

Sybella barely managed a nod of her skeleton head, "Yes," she whispered.

Ashrek leaned over the bed and poured the remainder of the water on her face, watching as she flicked her tongue in a vain attempt to gather even one drop.

"You are a liar. You defy me at every turn, why should I listen to anything you say?" He traced the anklet he had embedded into her leg. He had it placed there after the last time she tried to transport herself away. It was made of a special metal that could not be spelled. If she tried to leave, it would remain behind… and her leg with it. "I have everything I need now. Your people follow me wholeheartedly. The manor is mine. The tunnel is completed and the trade route open. You have nothing to offer me but your death. But come now, you still have the opportunity to be useful in the end."

Ashrek allowed the hounds to creep closer to the bed. They caught the scent of death and growled. Saliva dripped from their maws in anticipation. Just when he was about to release them, he heard one word.

"What did you say?"

"B-b-b-a-a-b-y."

Ashrek laughed. "Really, you and I both know you are *not* with child."

He watched her summon all her energy for her final plea,

"C-c-ould b-b-e."

Ashrek had to pause a moment. She was right. She was not with child *now*, but she could be. And a son could be the final authentication to his claim to power. He could ensure the continuation of his line and of course the child would be very powerful with their blood mixing and flowing in his veins. For the first time in weeks he looked at her with something other than loathing. How had he not thought of that himself? He allowed his power to flow, just enough for some color to come back into her cheeks. Sybella took a full breath of air for the first time in days, gasping as her chest rose and fell several times before she continued.

"Thank you, Lord Ashrek. I will not only carry your child but I have the power to ensure a boy is born, one that is more powerful than you can imagine. Only let me live, please."

"If you speak the truth how soon could you make this happen?"

"I need to visit my spell room for the necessary herbs, and then require your presence, only one night, during the full moon."

"The full moon is one week away." He let his power flow a bit more and watched as her cheeks filled in and her hair took on a luster it had never had in the past. "Do not get overly comfortable my dear. I still hold your life in the palm of my hand, and should you get any ideas…"

"I won't, I pro…..aaaahhhh!" She screamed as her other leg cracked loudly and twisted unnaturally between her knee and ankle. "I WON'T! I WON'T! I WON'T!"

"Just an insurance policy, my dear. You do not need to walk upright to bear a child. I'll have someone fashion a walking stick for you."

Ashrek left her writhing in pain, locking the door on his way out.

Chapter 8

AUNI LEAPED INTO THE AIR from the loft of the barn and circled above the small house, the moonlight bathed his jewel-colored wings in silver. All the human inhabitants were sound asleep.

'Naia, I need to speak with you.'

Naia exited the cottage and stretched, yawning so wide every sharp tooth was exposed, her claws made small divots in the soft earth.

'Yes Auni. What is it?'

'The time of the prophecy is at hand. I must cross the desert and find her.' Auni landed on the fence as he spoke.

'I have wondered if you thought so. I am in agreement. I will let the other packs know to be on guard. A great battle is coming, we must all be prepared.'

'Yes, the wind whispers to me. The time is late and He is closer than we think. It should take me a few days to reach her dwelling, pray she is in a good mood.'

'The One be with you.'

'And you.'

Auni took flight into the inky blue-black skies heading for the desert, while Naia loped off into the dense darkness of the woods.

When dawn broke, Elainea called for Naia with no response.

"Alric, have you seen Naia this morning?"

"No, now that I think of it, I haven't. Perhaps she is with Akronius at the river."

Akronius walked up the path, shivering in the brisk air, he quickly toweled his hair before the daily dropping temperature could freeze his locks. "No, she was not with me. She might have left with Auni last night. He spoke of a prophecy coming true, and that he had a part to play in it. Perhaps Naia had to go as well." He considered placing the towel across the small gate to dry but knew the cold air would hinder that, tossing it just inside near the open door he stretched his arms above his head, bracing on one of the house posts as Elainea scowled at him as she picked up the discarded item.

"Did he mention what the prophecy was about? Or who?" Kaison asked, stepping out into the dawning sunlight.

"No, he said only that your return meant it had begun. He said he would be gone several days, but did not mention where he was off to or that Naia would be going as well."

"Well, animals have their own ways of doing things." Kaison said, as he glanced around at the group. "We have things to accomplish as well. But, let's begin with breakfast!"

Elainea rolled her eyes and the men laughed as they followed her back inside, to the table, where they had a quiet meal. The question of what 'it' could be occupied all their thoughts and the prospects of battle weighed heavily on them all.

"So, what's the plan? What do we do now?" Elainea looked around the table noticing, not for the first time, that she was the only woman in their group; it didn't bother her outside of being the primary cook, maid and general caretaker of everyone. OK, maybe it did bother her a little. "Alric?"

"We haven't discussed plans yet but we all know Alanna's dying wish was to see me take my place on the throne. Of course, that was before we knew you were still alive. So, we do have options now. Despite that, Wleia raised us to believe in The One, in justice and love. We have to give the people HOPE again, give them the opportunity to live a life of peace without the threat of darkness creeping into their doors to steal their daughters."Alric hesitated before continuing, "We were also raised to believe no one is too far gone to be redeemed. Look at Akronius. Perhaps, we can find a way to save David as well. He is family."

The final statement was met with silence and then "The things I have heard from the townspeople get more and more troubling each day. Prisoners are going missing from the dungeons all the time. It is believed that the man you call family is allowing his Oracle Chumbra, to experiment on them. Redemption is available to all, Alric, but you have to WANT to be redeemed."

Kaison made a point of meeting Alric's eyes, "I understand how you feel Alric, you will have to be much stronger to face this kind of enemy, and I do not mean with just your gifts, you will need to harden your heart as well. Beyond that, they will have an army of soldiers standing between you. Men who have trained and fought for longer than you've been alive. Men and women trained by Akronius. They will not hold back. They will show no mercy. We will need more than just this small group, if we are to stand a chance at getting you even remotely close to the King."

Alric's shoulders slumped as he slouched down in his chair.

"What training have you had so far?" Kaison asked, glancing between Alric and Elainea.

"We've had no military training, if that's what you're asking." Alric mumbled, "Shama helped us gain a strong grip on our gifts, individually and together. I can channel Elainea's fire and she can use my sight. With some practice I am sure we could access the full range of gifts we each hold."

"That is wonderful," Kaison said, trying to soften the dejection he sensed in his son. "But you will need to start training in hand-to-hand combat as well. Do you have a sword?"

Elainea looked at Alric and smiled, receiving only a half-hearted smirk in response. "We should go outside." Everyone followed her into the yard and waited for whatever she had in mind.

Elainea took a deep breath and held her hand by her side. Flames sprouted from her fingertips and grew until they became the shape of a slender, sharply pointed rapier. She twirled it and went through a series of positions she had seen the men do during practice. She looked at Akronius for direction, her scarlet eyebrow raised in silent challenge as her hair rippled around her in the cool breeze.

"Well, that will certainly do." Akronius said, a broad smile causing the scars across his face to pucker. Quickly retrieving his double-edged long-sword, he approached her. "Is it only flame or can the little girl attack with it as well?"

He brought his sword toward her. Sparks flew as she countered his strike with her own. Akronius nodded in approval. Walking around her he observed and instructed her. "Widen your stance, grasp the pommel like this, use your hips, put your whole body into each strike." Over and over he took her through a series of stances, attacks and defenses until they both dripped with sweat. "Well done Elainea. But you will need to increase your endurance if you intend to keep the flame for an entire battle. We will get you an actual sword as well."

Breathing heavily Elainea smiled wide, she felt so alive! Her muscles ached; her right hand trembled from the exertion of keeping the magic flowing while countering Akronius' strikes. She let the flame go out as she stretched her fingers. She stood next to Kaison who clapped her on the shoulder with pride. She would show them she was more than a maid, she would fight with, and better than, any man.

Akronius turned to see Alric watching sullenly from the side. "Alric, you're not going to let your sister best you, now are you? Show us what you can do."

Meeting Akronius' eyes, a smirk quickly replaced the scowl as he masked his true thoughts. "Not intentionally of course, I have unsuccessfully tried forming a sword from my shielding abilities. I can borrow her flame and form a small dagger, but even that I cannot hold for as long as Elainea is able to. I seem to have only defensive abilities while my sister is the more violent one." Though he said this with a wink in her direction, there was a bitter note in his tone, and it was clear it was something he had thought long about and it bothered him.

Akronius had observed him silently before offering his thoughts. "Defense is useful in battle, Alric. Though it can be undermined by self-pity." He saw the boy flinch and knew his words had their desired effect. "Seeing where the threat is can prevent loss of life. Do not underestimate yourself just yet. Here, use my sword to go through some training drills." Akronius tossed it to Alric, the sun glinted off its blade and a blinding light flashed the moment his hand caught it causing everyone to shield their eyes and look away. When sight had been restored to them all, Alric stood as still as a statue, hand gripping the etched hilt, his eyes white and fixated onto the blade.

"ALRIC!" Elainea screamed, panic flushing her face as she tried to rush to his side, but was caught by the waist and pulled away by Kaison.

"Do not touch him!" He said harshly. "He is having a vision. His mother often fell into these trances. He will come to when The One is through with him."

Men in full suits of armor surrounded a figure standing atop a small knoll. A flaming sword was raised above his head and a battle cry sounded from his open lips. His armor bearer held a white banner with red edges, a great bird in its center. Several other banners waved in the distance. A crimson banner streaked through with black lightning and a deep green banner with golden filigree. Each banner circled the men in opposite directions, a darkness overshadowing them. For a moment, a face could be seen, blood-red eyes and a jagged mouth lined with rows of sinister teeth.

It seemed the small band of soldiers would be overpowered, the banners growing closer and closer to them, when from the mountains a roar sounded. Not a single roar, but the roar of a thousand voices united. The man smiled and pointed his sword at the nearest banner, the crimson one.

"ATTACK!"

Chapter 9

TAKING A DEEP BREATH ALRIC bent at the waist, bracing his hands on his knees as he looked around. Elainea was reaching for him, her face etched with fear. Kaison reached for her, his fingertips barely brushing hers. Akronius still had his arm raised from when he had tossed the sword, his face a mask of self-confidence. Having regained his breath, Alric stood and looked more closely at the sword he held, noticing a red gem like a ruby in the center of the hilt that pulsed and glowed brightly. He looked around at his companions once more, and saw minute movements. Kaison now had Elainea's clothes gripped in his hand and Akronius' face had morphed into confusion. He had somehow managed to slow time around him! Still clutching the sword, he walked toward Elainea. He could see the terror in her eyes, fear for him. He looked at Kaison, understanding and awe reflected back to him, while Akronius looked on with uncertainty. He laughed at the sudden turn of events. Maybe The One had finally heard his prayers for greater strength. He could use this weapon and finally be the man everyone wanted him to be. Walking inside the home he sat at the table, which was still covered with leftovers from their morning meal. The more he thought about it, the more he was sure it was meant to be. No one would be able to stop him; pounding his fist on the table in triumph he knocked a cup over, spilling its contents. Glancing at the spilled milk his stomach rumbled, although it had only been a short time since they broke their fast he was ravenous! Looking to his side, where he had laid the sword on the table, he tentatively reached for the gem and brushed his thumb across it, watching the pulsing first slow and then disappear.

"ALRIC!" Elainea cried out. "Where did he go? You said it was only a vision! Where did he go?" The panic was evident in her voice as she accused Kaison. She ran in one direction and then the other, looking for her brother who had vanished into thin air.

"I do not know. This never happened with Alanna. I do not understand." Kaison felt the blood drain from his face; he had no explanation for this. He had never seen nor heard of this happening to his wife during a vision.

"Relax! I am here, inside." Alric called with a smile in his voice, his tone full of pride.

Elainea rushed inside, her hair whipping behind her, "How? What? Really? You're eating again?" Her fear turned to incredulity as she watched her brother grin and place another piece of bread in his mouth.

"I'm famished! Whatever that was really wiped me out." Alric said, with his mouth full and his eyes twinkling.

Placing a steadying hand on Elainea's shoulder, Kaison stepped around her into the room. "You don't realize that you just had a vision? You said you had the gift of sight. How could this be your first vision?"

"I do have sight. But you know there are different manifestations of that gift, up until now, it was only for seeing great distances and through objects cloaked in magic." Alric took a sip of milk and cleared his throat as he looked at his father. "Ask… I know you want to." He said with a mischievous grin.

"How did you do it?" Akronius asked before anyone else could.

Alric looked at the double-edged long-sword lying near him on the table and placed his hand on the leather-bound handle, just shy of grazing the now dormant stone that lay in the pommel. "I believe this triggered the vision, but *I* triggered something else entirely. Do you see this gem?" Everyone leaned closer to inspect the object he was pointing at. "It was glowing when I came out of the vision and time seemed to have slowed around me. I could see Kaison grabbing you, Elainea, and Akronius' hand was still raised from throwing the sword, but I could move around you all with no detection. It was amazing!"

Kaison's jaw dropped in surprise. "No, it can't be." He moved closer to inspect the sword. "It is!"

Turning to Akronius with hard eyes he asked, "Where did you get this sword?"

"Wleia gave it to me," Akronius answered, meeting the hard stare with one of his own. "She said it had been passed down in her family for generations. She'd intended to pass it to Alric when the time came. Why? What is it?"

"This sword…" Kaison closed his eyes briefly, and breathed deeply before looking his son in the eye. "This is King Vernis's sword.

Do you know of him?"

"Not very much," Alric said with a shrug. "He was a powerful king, who fought many battles. He disappeared after the battle of Eckter."

"He was more than just a powerful king," Kaison said, again reminded of how little of his own history Alric knew, having grown up without him to impart that knowledge because of his manipulative and murderous sister. "He was a brilliant captain. The way we train as soldiers is still based on his tactics. He was strategic and cunning. No one could understand how he knew the things he did." Looking down at the blade again with a nod he continued, "But, I suppose we have an idea now. If he was able to slow time around him, there would be no limit to where he could sneak into, or information he could gather. Amazing! This sword could be the advantage we need against that pretender to the throne, David!"

"Exactly what I was thinking Father." Alric said strongly, sitting up at the table. "This will help me get close enough to kill him. Not just him, but Chumbra as well. No one will be able to stop me!"

"That is all true, but you will still need additional training. A weapon is only as strong as the man or woman that wields it," Kaison nodded. "But how did Wleia come to have it? She was not of noble blood, was she?" Kaison asked, turning to look at Elainea.

Elainea sighed and lowered herself into an empty chair. "Not that I am aware. She told me my father died in the flash floods the season before my birth. Her twin brother died as well. We have no more information than that. What happened to King Vernis?"

"It is a mystery." Akronius said, taking up where Kaison had stopped. "As soldiers we were taught about him mainly for his tactical prowess, but all that is said is that during the last battle he was outnumbered and surrounded, with the sea at his back. Then with no warning the enemy retreated after having learned their general had been killed. No one could understand how, but seeing how this sword works, we can guess now. Right after this battle, Vernis disappeared. He did not celebrate with his men. He never returned to Nuru Manor. He simply vanished."

"Akronius said your mother had this sword passed down in her family for generations, is there no one left who may know of its origin?" Kaison asked Elainea again, "You are sure?"

"Yes, I'm sure, and no, unfortunately she was the last of her line.

Her twin brother had not married and had no children. We are the last of our line.”

The small group sat in silence, each lost in their own thoughts before Akronius broke it.

“We should continue your training Alric, you too Elainea. Try not to touch that gem.”

Chapter 10

ALRIC AND ELAINEA LIMPED TOWARD the riverbank with aching muscles after being pushed hard by both Kaison and Akronius.

"You are very good at training them, Akronius," Kaison said as he cleaned his dagger. "I remember now why you were made captain of the guard at such a young age. You were ruthless then." Kaison glanced over to see Akronius round his shoulders and lower his eyes. "But now your sharp edges seemed to have been smoothed down. You seem calmer, focused. What caused the change?"

"I'm glad the change is visible to you. You're right, I was ruthless, and with good reason. Do you know how I came to be in your service?"

"No, nothing beyond the captain coming back with a boy who was near death. Another mouth to feed, another body to train."

"That is true." Akronius sat on a stump of wood and raked his hands through his sweat soaked hair, his eyes lifting and gazing at the mountains in the distance. "Violence has been a part of my life from my earliest memory. My parents were slaughtered by vagrants as they traveled into the city for trade during my seventh year. If I think hard enough, I can still hear the animalistic roar my father made as we watched the blade cross my mother's throat. I can smell the metallic scent of blood wafting from the corpses as they lay on the side of the road. I spent several days there beside our burned-out wagon before a battalion of your guards found me." Akronius looked up into Kaison's eyes. "I was told the look on my young face would haunt the men for a lifetime, and despite their best efforts, I did not speak for a year. Instead, I learned how to wield a sword and track anything living. When I was ten, I set out in the middle of the night and it was two weeks before I returned. But when I did, I was covered in the blood of those murderers and ready to complete my initiation into the guard. So, to say I was ruthless is an understatement. I was Death! I was a blunt object Devona used to beat others with, until she sent me to find your son. In searching for him, I found myself, or more accurately, The One found me. Wleia changed my perception and my fate."

Kaison silently watched Akronius. "That is some tale. If I am correct, I was twenty and had just become King when you were brought to us. How old were you when you became captain of the guard?"

"I was only eighteen, the youngest in Elhaanai history. I was successful at every mission, and killed more men than I care to admit. Devona saw the wounds behind my eyes and nurtured the pain. I even suspect she had the previous captain killed in order to keep me within her control. Your sister convinced me that you were a weak leader, and had me watch you for a very long time," Akronius said with obvious regret.

"That does not surprise me. I do not blame you. It turns out that my sister was very troubled. Alanna knew it. She tried to get me to see, but I would not, could not. Devona and I had been close as children, and I married young. I suppose that was partially the reason we drifted apart as the years went on. Devona was only fifteen when she was given to an older man in a political match, while I was allowed to marry for love at seventeen." Kaison sighed, he'd not thought of his little sister without hatred in so long, it pained him to do so now.

Sensing his unease, Akronius tried to steer the conversation. "We're all a product of our choices, you could no more save Devona than you could have saved me or your wife. I am coming to learn that The One has a mysterious way about Him. Just when we think we know what His plan is, it changes."

"Well said Akronius, I see you made use of the manor library when you had the time. You were always more than just a blunt object. You were and still are a man with a predestined purpose; you just needed to see it for yourself." Kaison stood and stretched, stopping just short of entering the home. He turned and leaned against the doorpost. "How did you receive your gift? You were ordinary when I last saw you, lethal, but ordinary."

Akronius smiled. "I tracked the twins from here to the mountains, found them and Shama high up there," gesturing to the mountains in the distance, "Shama somehow helped cleanse me. I entered a pool and came out different. I don't fully understand it myself, but he said I could go back to finish my training. This gift is both not what I would have expected and more, if that makes sense."

"Yes, it does," Kaison smiled. "Not what I would have expected for you either, but here we are. I can help with your training as I said.

You already know how to speak with the animals around you, and you are able to channel some of their senses, but there is much more. Once you are strong enough you will be able to shape-shift. My familiar and I often hunted and flew together. I could shift fully into a falcon and partially into several other creatures. It takes great focus and stamina, but I think you are up to the task."

Akronius grinned with sudden anticipation.

"What was it like?" Elainea asked as she sat on the river bank and watched Alric rinse his hands in the flowing water. She wrapped her arms around herself to stave off the cold, winter's tendrils were creeping down the mountainside and would have them in its grip before long.

He paused a moment before answering, "It was like standing in the middle of this river and feeling it flow around me but never really touching me. I could move in it but wasn't quite a part of it. It was amazing!"

"This could be just what we need for you to get close to David and…" Elainea paused; she didn't want to say it.

"Kill him? Yeah, we all think it but no one has actually said it yet. Is that what I am meant to do? Kill my own cousin? Is that the right thing? Is it our only option? I know what Kaison and Akronius think, but maybe I can make him see how wrong he is, how his rule is hurting our people and killing our land. Maybe he will listen."

"And if he won't?" Elainea couldn't meet his eyes. She knew her brother wasn't a killer. He was the joker, the one who wanted everyone to be full and happy.

"I don't know."

Chapter 11

SYBELLA HOBBLED DOWN THE DARK hallway, leaning heavily on the stick Ashrek had sent to her after he broke her leg, the tap, tap, tap of its end echoing in her ears. She was not a tall woman but the poor excuse for a staff barely reached her hip, forcing her to hunch over. Her leg dragged slightly with each step. Tap, scratch, tap, scratch. She was a beautiful crone.

"Can't you walk any faster Woman?" Ashrek shouted impatiently over his shoulder. "I have better things to do than watch you drag your crippled leg around after me."

"I am sorry, My Lord. The staff you so generously provided is somewhat short, and my leg has not quite healed. I am not at my full strength." Sybella exaggerated her shuffle. The insufferable man could wait for an eternity for all she cared. "The servants must have forgotten to bring my meal last night and this morning, so I am..."

"I do not care about your discomforts!" Ashrek hissed as they arrived at their destination. "Go, inside. I promised you access to your spell room, so go do what you said and you had better not disappoint me. None of your extremities are necessary to bring my son into this world."

Sybella dipped her head. "Yes My Lord, I will mix the ingredients needed that will guarantee the birth of a strong son." She shrank in on herself, curving her shoulders to look smaller, weaker. "May I make one request, please?"

"You may ask," he scoffed. "But I am neither inclined nor am I under any obligation to grant you anything."

"As you wish My Lord, I understand. Could you please have a servant bring me a small meal while I work on the potion? It will greatly help with my focus to complete this task for you quickly."

The whole time she kept her eyes downcast, hands clutching the short stick, until her knuckles were white. It took all the effort she had. She was still too weak and dependent on this cruel man who had killed her father. She knew her husband waited for the day he could feed her to his hounds. Inside, she seethed with hatred and the need for revenge.

Ashrek stepped closer to her and raised her head with one finger until their eyes met. "Hungry, are you?" His warm breath brushed against her pale skin, causing chills to raise bumps under the malicious tone of his words. "But for what? I can sense the hatred you try so hard to hide, the way you hold that stick when you would like nothing more than to scratch my eyes out." He wiped an angry tear that had leaked from the corner of her eye and smiled. "You may think you will have your revenge but you can dispense with that hope right now. As soon as your usefulness has ended so will your life. But, for now, I'll have someone bring you a meal… something special, just for you." He patted her cheek and turned for the door, leaving a guard posted outside the room.

Sybella hobbled over to her work table, lightly placing her hand in the center she spoke quietly until a soft click was heard and a drawer slipped open on the side. She withdrew her spell book and flipped to the first page. She read the inscription quietly, her voice rising as she hobbled from one corner of the room to another a dark mist emerged from its pages and settled around the room. Reaching the pinnacle of the chant she slammed the book shut, power rippling out from where she stood once more in the center of the room and slammed the mist against the walls. Once the mist had cleared entirely, she picked up a cup and threw it at the door, when the guard didn't enter she knew the spell had worked. Placing her stick down she grabbed the sides of the table and screamed, the rage bubbled from her belly and she shook from the force of it. She would have her revenge and it would start now. Grabbing the stick, she had been given and a rock that looked decorative, she held them together and whispered another incantation. The stick grew and merged with the stone until it was a strong staff infused with the darkness of the crystal hidden inside the rock, but, to anyone else it would still only look like a tree branch.

As she flipped through her book of spells, gathering the information needed for the birth of a son, a knock sounded at the door and a servant walked in with a food tray. "Mistress, your meal from Lord Ashrek." The tray rattled in his hands and he would not meet her eyes, she knew it would be something she would not enjoy.

"Thank you," she said, watching a bead of sweat drip down his green tinged face and his throat work hard to swallow past a lump caught there. He set the tray down and tripped over his own feet as he fled from the room, leaving the platter placed precariously on the table. Approaching it with caution, Sybella lifted the tray cover, dropping the lid with a clang as she covered her mouth and gagged at the smell that wafted into her face. One of the hounds lay curled in on itself, its tail and legs tucked under it as if it slept on a bed of green lettuce, the slit in its throat and the apple stuffed in its mouth the only indication it was a sleep it would never wake from. She pried the apple from its jaws, turning it around to a place not marked by teeth. She took a bite, "Let us begin."

Chapter 12

LORD ALCHERIST STUDIED HIS SLEEPING son in the moonlight shadows of clouds drifting across the cage bars. His brain worked through what Elmeera had told him. She claimed something was wrong with their child, he was different…. evil, she'd said. What happened during his captivity? What had they done to his son! His fists clenched until his knuckles cracked. He could hear his teeth grinding as he tried to control his anger. Exiting the room, he made his way down the candlelit hall to where his wife lay sleeping. Flickering flames danced sinisterly across the stone walls. Standing over her in the darkness he could see that her eyes were sunken into her skull, and her hair was streaked with premature gray strands. Her skin was waxy and without the blush her age should have provided. She stirred restlessly, mumbling incoherently, as her hands clawed and grasped the bedsheets at her sides. Across her chest the outline of the red tinted scraps of bandages were visible beneath her nightgown. They covered bite marks from nursing their son. Her maid had tried to dissuade her from repeatedly feeding him, but in her desperation to make up for the time lost she had persisted. The wounds now festered, causing her current state of malaise.

Despite seeing the evidence with his own eyes, he couldn't believe it. He wouldn't believe it! This child had been a miracle. After years of emptiness, he would rather die than let that evil family be the reason his bloodline was doomed to disappear from the pages of history. He would find a cure, even if it meant entering the very bowels of hell to find it! He would do whatever it took to save his son.

Alcherist let the sheer curtains fall around his wife's bed, standing there for a moment longer, watching her shaky breathing rattle her body, before turning abruptly toward the door. Elmeera was barely a ghost of the woman he loved so desperately. He headed toward a dark set of stairs that lead down into the belly of his manor, a place that was forbidden to everyone, and all but forgotten by most. He had come upon it by chance as a child with his brother during a game of hide and seek, now he used it to hide his deeds, and seek out a cure.

As he reached the bottom of the stairs, what had been soft echoes became reverberating screams. Entering the decaying doorway, he saw a woman strapped to a table. Blood soaked through her restraints from dozens of cuts on her arms. Her eyes rolled beneath swollen and discolored lids, which had sunken into what once may have been a beautiful face. Her body arched from the table in pain as another cut was made across her exposed thigh.

Alcherist calmly approached the table and ran his hand down the side of her bruised face, mocking her with his show of tenderness. "This could all be over. I can put a stop to this torture right now. All you have to do is tell me where to find Shama. I know your people basically worship him. Tell me and this all ends, right now. How do I find this Oracle?"

He'd heard whispers of this great Oracle; they claimed he was a shaman and a healer. There were rumors that he could communicate directly with The One. Even thinking of that... that, name, caused his mouth to twist in disgust. If *He* was real, He should have prevented all of this. If *He* was all-powerful and so loving He should have protected his wife and son. He spat, as if doing so could erase the bitterness from his mouth, at the thought of saying it aloud. No, he did not believe, but he would bleed this mystical man dry if it meant his son would be healed.

The woman started whispering, her swollen lips moving rapidly. Alcherist bent close to hear her words.

"Blessed be The One who hears the suffering of His children. He who attends to the needs of His sons and daughters. Blessed be The One who lays claim to vengeance for their sake. Blessed be The One who bestows blessings and loves us first, last, and always. Blessed be..."

"SHUT UP!" Her head whipped to the side as he slapped her once and then again and again. "SHUT UP! SHUT UP! SHUT UP!" Though no sound came out, her lips still moved and her eyes slit open slightly, taking on a distant look before glazing over in white and opening fully.

Turning to him, she said in a strong steady voice that was not her own. "You seek for what you do not understand. You cannot steal what would be freely given. Hear me, turn from your path and find freedom." The last word spoken was barely a whisper, as life left her body.

"AAARRRGGGHHH!" Alcherist screamed his rage into the darkness of the dungeon. The guard shrinking into the corner in fear of retribution for yet another girl's death, listening to the wet squelching sound as Alcherist repeatedly drove his fist into the stone wall until his hand bled.

"Go into the city and get me another," Alcherist said shoulders heaving, his breath coming in short gasps.

"But, My Lord, this is the fifth girl! The villagers are starting to whisper, they say that what is happening in the villages around Nuru Manor has found its way here. All the girls, they all say the same thing, My Lord, the last words never change. Perhaps you should…"

CRACK!

The guard's head snapped back and connected with the wall as Alcherist's bloody fist met and broke his nose. "I don't pay you to think or suggest what I should do! You are a tool, a slave to my will, and just as replaceable as that slab of meat on the table! Go, find, ANOTHER!"

The man scurried from the room, blood flowing over the hand that clutched the shattered part of his face. Alcherist turned to the table, where just like the previous victims, the woman's face had taken on a peaceful glow. Growling in disgust and frustration he unstrapped the body, took a handful of hair and pulled her from the table. Her body flopped limply behind him as he turned and heaved her to the floor. Dragging her down the hall, a path of dried blood showed the way to a pit where he threw her and watched her fall to join the other believers of The One. All their voices echoed in these walls, "Blessed be The One… Blessed be The One…" He sank to his knees, clutched the edge of the pit and screamed into the abyss. First his brother's misguided plans, then the kidnapping and return of his damaged child and then his nephew stealing the revenge from him. No matter how hard he tried to hold it, he felt his control slipping through his fingers like oil. He sat in the darkness, surrounded with the scent of death for hours, soaking in his pain and misery.

"My Lord I… I am sorry. It is late in the day and everyone is behind locked doors. I could not find anyone for you." Alcherist could see the man's pulse racing in his throat, blood pumping furiously with terror and leaking from a crooked nose beneath wide terror-filled eyes. Closing his own eyes, he could almost smell his fear, acrid and sulfurous. Sulfur, that was it.

"Have no fear." Alcherist said with a smile. "We'll not need another. No, we need someone else entirely."

He stood up so abruptly that the man stumbled back, and without thinking twice, Alcherist reached forward to steady him, then used his counterweight to throw the man over and into the same pit he had been studying moments ago. The look of gratitude quickly changed to horror as the man's scream was cut short as he fell to his death.

"We need the devil herself."

Chapter 13

NAIA RAN THROUGH THE NIGHT and the next day before resting beside a small lake to enjoy the small rabbit she had flushed out from the overgrown brush. Having finished her meal, she walked to the water's edge for a drink. Her lapping caused gentle ripples in the water, settling to reveal a full moon surrounded by an endless display of stars. As she gazed up, she felt a pressure rising in her chest, causing her to pant rapidly. She did not understand it, but remembered the last time she had felt it.

"AAAHHHOOOO!" Throwing her head back she howled to the heavens, with her eyes closed she could feel the vibrations deep inside her. As the last notes faded, her eyes opened to see a soft glow beside her on the shoreline. Cocking her head to the side, she inspected the light before her; different but not threatening.

"Naia?" A voice said from within the light.

'Who are you?'

"You know who I am, Naia."

'Yes. What do you want from me?'

"You are close to your destination. The other packs are nearing even now. You will have to prove yourself to them before they will trust your word regarding the prophecy."

'What would you have me do?' Naia realized who she was speaking with. She was humbled that He deemed her worthy of His presence and excited at what it meant. The prophecy was true!

"You are a dire wolf. A noble breed. You will have to go against your nature and submit to the pack. They will be difficult to convince. When the time comes, trust your heart. Do not force any to follow you. Be steadfast and unmovable in this task. You have my blessing."

The light dimmed and once again she was alone and felt the pressure rising within her.

"AAAHHHOOOO!"

Only this time, several voices answered her. The hairs on the back of her neck stood up and her tail went rigid. Growls sounded from the darkness. Like she had been instructed, she fought the urge to bare her teeth and growl back.

From the darkness, four sets of amber eyes and one of green approached her slowly.

'To whom do you belong and why are you in our territory?'

Fighting the need to roll her eyes she replied. *'I am Naia and I BELONG to no one. I am here to speak to the pack leaders about an urgent matter.'*

'Rogues are not welcome here. You would do well to leave. You will not be extended the same allowance twice.' Several menacing growls emphasized his meaning. Naia glanced around her, ill at ease but confident.

'I will leave once my task is complete and not before. Are you the Alpha?'

'If you don't value your own life, neither will I!' He growled and sprang forward. Instinctively she wanted to go on the attack as well, and her muscles tensed in response. But again she remembered the words spoken to her. As he tackled her to the forest floor, she exposed her throat and whined softly enough that only he would hear. She felt his teeth pierce her flesh, not enough to draw blood but to make a point nevertheless. As his saliva coated her fur he shook her once and then paused.

Releasing her, he stepped back, licked his jaws and sat on his haunches. *'You are willing to die for this message?'*

Naia stayed where he had released her and looked up at him. *'YES.'*

He was silent for a moment, appraising her and the situation. *'Very well. Follow me.'*

She rose and followed behind the small pack, thanking The One for His guidance and trust.

Chapter 14

IT WAS DAWN WHEN THEY reached the dire wolf den. Naia glanced around in awe. There were so many! It had been a very long time since she'd caught the scent of humans, so she knew this must be a safe place. They had settled into the crags of the mountain range nearest the desert. The heat that wafted in from the dunes along with the cool air from the mountain created a perfect habitat for them. A small pool, fed by the runoff of the mountain's frozen peak, gave them water and the forest provided the rest. As Naia entered further into their home, she could feel eyes on her from every direction. Pups, who were bravest dared a few paces closer to her only to receive warning snaps and low growls from watchful mothers as they were herded back and deep into their dens. She followed the large male as he led her up the rocks to a vantage point and told her to wait. She didn't have to wait long.

'I am Mkuu, Alpha of this pack.' Mkuu confidently stepped out from the mouth of the cave. A powerful aura emanated from him causing Naia to instinctively lower her head. *'Say what you have come to say and leave.'*

Naia was sure she looked like a pup before him. The top of her ears barely reached his muzzle and everything in her wanted to cower lower to the floor. His fur was the color of midnight and his eyes like ice as he watched her. She'd never been around so many of her kind and wasn't sure what to do or say. She knew her life was forfeit if she offended or appeared threatening to them, as if she could. A slight breeze ruffled her fur, and with it a warmth and voice inside that simply said, *"REMEMBER."* She took a deep breath, lifted her head slightly and began.

'Long ago a prophecy was told of a Man King who would die and return. This King would be blessed with a powerful connection to animals. It is said he'll return to rid the world of its evil inclinations, bringing unity to all. We would no longer be hunted for our pelts and blood, tooth and claw, but once again revered and honored. All will revert to worshiping The One as it was intended from the beginning. But to do so, will require a great war in which we all must fight. I have

come to ask for your assistance in this fight. The King has returned! I have seen him with my own eyes. Even now a Firauni, who was also present at his return, believes as I do, and is headed into the desert to gather more forces. Will you join us?'

Mkuu gazed at her in silence for a long time. *'Why should we help mankind? They have hunted us to near extinction. They wear the furs of our mothers, our brothers, our pups. They bleed us dry and grind our bones for their own evil purposes. We owe them nothing.'* He spoke matter-of-factly, not with anger or malice. He genuinely had no reason to help or agree to her cause. He glanced at Nguvu briefly before returning his focus to Naia.

'All you say is true, Alpha. We owe THEM nothing, but we owe The One EVERYTHING. Were you not led to this safe place by Him? Has he not provided food and water and shelter for you and your young? Look at how many you have! You may be thriving, but you are in hiding here. Don't you want the pups to learn the freedom of running for the joy of it and not from fear? We once roamed the woods on the other side of the river freely, and we should once again, it's our land. Help me take it back.'

Mkuu looked at her without revealing his thoughts, before stepping closer. Naia wanted to step back from him, but to do so would be a sign of weakness. *'Who are you?'* He asked, as he took a deep breath, filling his nose with her scent.

'I am Naia.' She replied softly.

He stepped back. *'Follow me.'*

'Mkuu do you think that wise? She is a rogue and we don't know if what she says is…'

'Gggggggrrrrrrrrrrrrrrrrr'

'My apologies, Alpha. You know best. I will wait for you to call for me.' The growl that came from the alpha sent Naia and the other wolf, who must have been his beta, to their knees in submission. He continued into the cave without a backwards glance to see if Naia was following, he knew she was, there was no other option.

Naia tried to hide the tremors rippling over her body, but knew she failed. The further into the cave system they walked, the more she feared. He could kill her at any time and no one would or could stop him. Finally, they reached a small pool fed by a trickle of water from the top of the cave. Mkuu took a small drink before reclining nearby.

'Sit with me, don't be afraid little one. I know who you are. The moment I scented you I remembered you, and your mother.'

50

'*You knew my mother? Me? But how?*' Naia lowered herself unceremoniously onto the rock floor.

'*Your mother was part of our pack long ago. We adopted her when she was just a pup. We found her wounded and alone, her own pack having been slaughtered by men. She was not a dire wolf, but at that time we were not quite as selective as we are now. She thrived with us and mated one of our own. From that bond a pup was born, Nguvu. She was pregnant when tragedy struck. We had been out for a hunt and a strange black wolf crossed our path. He had been hunting and killing the animals of men. Your father killed him, but did not survive his own wounds for long. Your mother, sadly, was separated from us in the ensuing chaos of being hunted for crimes we did not commit. We were forced into hiding and I believe rather than lead anyone to the pack, she sacrificed herself, remaining alone. I assume you were born sometime during those lost years.*'

'*I suppose so. My mother was killed by hunters. They thought she was killing their chickens. We were trying to get to the river, to cross to the woods. I was raised by a human woman. She was kind.*' Mkuu was silent as he watched Naia process the information she'd just learned. Her mother had chosen to live as a rogue rather than risk the lives of the entire pack, and here she was, asking them to do that very thing for humans who would not think twice about killing one of them.

'*I am truly sorry to hear that, but life must go on. Now, this prophecy you speak of. We also know of it, but most will not act on that knowledge. There are none here, save for the pups, who have not felt the loss of a pack mate from human hands. I will let each decide for themselves what they will do; they can choose to go with you or not. You will address the pack tonight and then go, with any who follow, to the other packs if more wolves are needed. I will have my second escort you to a resting place. NGUVU.*'

'*Yes Alpha.*' The brutish male that had brought her in stepped from the shadows and Naia thought her eyes would burst from her head. *He* was her brother!

Chapter 15

'NGUVU, ESCORT YOUR SISTER to a place where she can rest until tonight. She will be addressing the pack; any who choose to accompany her on this quest may do so.'

'As you wish Alpha.' He didn't even have the courtesy to look shocked. Leaving the cave, she glanced back and saw a twinkle in Mkuu's eye; she even thought she heard him chuckle. This was not funny. Her… brother, had almost killed her a few hours ago! Stopping at the base of the rocks, she waited until he looked her way.

'You KNEW! You attacked me at the lake, suggested I am untrustworthy and might attempt an attack on your alpha and all the while, you KNEW who I was! Why you little… little… UUUGGHHH!'

'Careful Sister, YOU are the little one here. And no, I didn't really know. When I bit you, you smelled familiar. Not enough to trust you instinctively, but enough not to kill you immediately.' He turned his back again and started walking toward a small den on the outskirts of their home. *'This is where I was born. Where our mother lived. You can stay here until tonight. I stay close to the alpha. If you need me, I will know.'*

'How?'

'Can't you feel it? Now that we are close, it is as if a tendril passed between us. I can sense you. And I can sense your anger,' he said with a smile. *'The longer you spend with us, the stronger you will feel the ties.'*

He cocked his head to the side as she began to circle him slowly. She inhaled his scent and observed him. He was larger than her but still not as big as the alpha. His dark fur had streaks of brownish red where hers was light grey; his eyes were deep amber while hers were sky blue. She wondered what their parents looked like; did they resemble them at all? Flipping her tail at him, she walked into the small den. It had been too long since her mother was here so her scent was gone. She'd hoped something, somehow had lingered. Her heart sank with that realization, nothing remained. She lay down, covered her face with her tail to sleep. In the corner of her mind she felt a small caress and sighed knowing her brother watched over her, even from a distance.

'Alpha, will you really allow the pack the choice to follow Naia?'

'Is there a reason I should not, Nguvu?' Mkuu asked jovially. *'Speak freely, no one can hear you question my authority.'* He knew Nguvu was young and headstrong. He wanted a pack of his own and whether he was aware of it or not, Mkuu had been training him for that since his birth. That time was now; the pack had become too large for one alpha. He had been unsure how to broach the subject in a way that would allow Nguvu to feel honored and not cast aside. The One had provided it now.

'No Mkuu, I don't doubt your wisdom. I know the prophecy as well as you, but the other packs will not be receptive of her message and she is... small. It would be easy to kill her, and then what would happen to the ones who followed her? It is dangerous, that is all I meant.'

Mkuu paced the length of the cave, his claws clicking on the stone and echoing in the silence. Dust particles floated in the dim light with each step as he appeared to be deeply considering Nguvu's words. *'You're right; her size will be seen as a weakness. What do you suggest?'*

'As much as it would pain me to part with you, I request to accompany her and any who choose to follow. I can teach her our ways and protect her, protect them all.'

'Spoken like a true Alpha. Come Nguvu, it is time to address our packs.'

They walked together, speaking quietly, until they reached the den where Naia was resting. They found her at the entrance watching the pups playing under the watchful eyes of their mothers.

'Come Naia, it is time to address the pack. We'll see who is willing to go with you to bring this prophecy to pass. Your brother will be going with you. Together, you will start a new pack. He will be your Alpha.'

Naia could see the pride in her brother's amber eyes, the way his shoulders went back and his chest puffed up just a little more as she listened to Mkuu convey his confidence in Nguvu's leadership abilities. It bristled her slightly to be under her brother's rules, she did not know him, she did not know this culture at all and would need to learn quickly. She fell in behind the two males as they headed to a nearby clearing. When they reached the center Mkuu stood silently, and slowly everyone started gathering. Naia could feel another tug in her mind and assumed that was his call to them. It was different from what she felt from Nguvu, more assertive. Once everyone was accounted for, he began to speak.

'This is Naia, she is the daughter of Binti; lost but now returned to us with news. Listen to her and decide for yourself, with my blessing, what you will do.'

He gave her a nod and stepped back.

'I am Naia. I have seen the fulfillment of the prophecy regarding the returned King. I have seen this King with my own eyes and have come to ask for your help in restoring the throne.' Naia watched her words settle over the pack, several eyes widened and though she was not linked to them she could imagine the conversations and questions bouncing across the mental threads as several shifted from paw to paw uncomfortably.

'Your wise Alpha has pointed out valid reasons why you may be hesitant to stand with me, with us. My own mother was killed by mankind, but I was also raised by them. I was loved by and mourned for a human woman when she died. But just like some wolves are evil, so are some men. We must be the ones to ensure the right King sits on the throne so we can regain our lands once more. Give our pups the opportunity to roam freely as we once did, as we were meant to by The One. I am asking you to accompany me and my brother Nguvu, to gather more wolves. We will need every claw and tooth to fight the rising evil. What will you decide? To live here in peace and in hiding, or to FIGHT for our freedom, FOR OUR FUTURE!' Naia made eye contact with as many wolves as she could before stepping back once more so their Alpha could speak.

Mkuu looked around at his pack, he could see the indecision and fear, and he could feel the doubt through his bond with them.

'You have heard her speak. We have all lost someone at the hands of mankind. But, The One created us powerful and free. I have stayed here with you out of my own fear, what we have is good and we have prospered here. Hiding here. Knowing that, I can say with conviction that we would be doing our creator a disservice by remaining as we are instead of as He intended us to be. We cannot all go, the young must be cared for and the pack must live beyond the ensuing battle, but those of you who wish to go, have my blessing. Your new Alpha will be Nguvu. You will follow and obey him as you have me.'

Silence filled the clearing as the pack contemplated Naia's and Mkuu's words. One by one several wolves stepped forward until they had a group of three males and two females willing to go with her. More than she had expected. Each one approached Nguvu and bared their necks, he bit them gently and then turned to her.

'You bit me already, Brother.'

Mkuu laughed genuinely this time. *'That was different, Naia. Nguvu must bite you now to assume his role as Alpha over you and create a bond that will claim you as his, deeper than a familial bond.'*

'Alright.'

She bared her neck to her brother and as he pierced her for the second time, she felt the bond snap into place. But not just with him, she felt the other members of this new pack as well. It was as if a piece that she hadn't even known was missing had been found. She felt whole!

'What now?' She asked her Alpha.

'Now we go find others willing to fight with us.' He turned toward Mkuu and bowed low. Rising, he howled into the sky and broke into a run. As she ran with her new pack, she heard the howls behind her in a sad but triumphant echo.

Chapter 16

THE DESERT LAY BEFORE HIM, vast, barren and acrid. Auni watched the wind lift and swirl sand from one dune to another. He knew food would be scarce, but more importantly water would be even harder to find. Auni sat in the shade of a tree facing the miles of wastelands that no man dared to travel. He didn't want to travel there, but he knew what his part in the prophecy was destined to be. He'd known of it all his life, even after so many years he could still hear his father's voice.

"Father, tell me the story again."

"Auni, you have heard that tale so often I'm sure you must have it memorized by now."

"Yes, but you tell it sooo much better! Tell me. Pleeeaaaassseee?"

"Alright, alright." Auni's father settled a large ruby colored wing over the small chick gazing up at him with wide green eyes. *"Before your little golden beak broke through your shell, our elder selected you from the hatchery. Out of hundreds of eggs the swirling colors on yours drew her eye. She said you were destined to help fulfill a great prophecy. You would help gather great warriors who would fight to place the rightful King on the throne of men. She said you would be strong enough to fly over the wasteland, further than any of our kind has gone before, your song will be your salvation and you will find the great dragon."*

"Wow. A real dragon." His tiny voice was filled with awe and trepidation. *"How will I know when the time is right Father? How will I know what to do or where to go?"* Auni trembled under his father's wing, who gazed lovingly down at him.

"The One will guide and protect you, my son. You only need to learn His voice so you can recognize it when the time comes. Can you do that?"

"Yes, Father. I can do that. I'm sure of it."

Shaking himself out of the reverie, he knew the time had come. He would travel as far as he could. Once night fell, it would be cooler. What he would do when the searing sun rose again, he could not say. He prayed The One would guide him. He watched the heavens for the star that would guide him to his ultimate destination.

Reminiscing on what his father told him, that he was chosen for this role by the elders of their flock, was momentarily pushed aside as other memories came to him. He tried not to ponder too much on them, but they demanded recognition. Hunted by mankind for sport and captivity, there were no more *flocks*, only a few individual Firauni remained. It had been years since he had come across another of his kind. His hope was that their numbers would increase with the return of the King, and in time, peace.

Glancing up once more, he could see the dark blue velvet of the night sky perforated with tiny dots of light, and there, the brightest of them all was the star that would lead him. One, and then another and another bloomed brighter before his eyes, revealing the path he would follow. His destination was far to the west, an oasis known only in Firauni lore. Auni picked a few more berries from a nearby branch before launching himself into the air.

He flew straight and true, the stars his only guide. The wind, his lone companion, lifted him in its currents and propelled him forward with speed. His mind jumped from the past to the future, what had been to what could be. His mate was lost to another, but hope was blossoming within him that he would find love again, perhaps even be blessed with chicks of his own. Lost in his reflective thoughts, time passed quickly. He glanced upwards and saw that he was still on course. Glancing below, he could see there was neither tree nor stone to land upon. He flew on until he could feel the sun's heat starting to crest the horizon behind him. He would have to find somewhere to rest soon. He scoured the terrain below him, watching his shadow coast over the warming sand and finally spotted a large skeleton near some jagged rocks. He was able to lift the skull with his talons and place it on the shaded side of the rocks. Tucking his beak beneath his wings, he rested inside the hollow space.

By the time dusk was once again upon him, he was exhausted despite having rested. He needed water and soon, the heat was unforgiving and draining him faster than he had anticipated. He could feel his feathers drying and becoming more and more brittle. The sun finally fell below the horizon. He set off once more, following the stars through another long night with only his thoughts for company. His eyes were glazing over and his wings felt weak as the moon set, one by one the stars faded away and the sun began its ascent into a peach sky.

Each flap took enormous effort, but he could not fail when he knew he was so close. Blinking, he could feel the coarse grains scratching beneath the membrane. There was something blocking his vision, he blinked again, but it did not clear. No, it was not in his eye... it was in the distance! A dark shadow grew larger with each moment. He would not rest this day; he flew on as the sun rose higher and higher and he sank lower and lower. He could feel his wings faltering, but to land in the sand would mean death. The sun was directly before him and the glare was blinding now. He tried to look away from the light but quickly became disoriented. Then he was falling, plummeting to the desert floor.

'HELP ME!' He screeched.

In response, he heard one word. *"SING."*

He hit the ground and felt the air rush out of him. He heard the crack of one wing as he bounced, landed on it and rolled, screeching in agony. *"SING FIRAUNI, SING!"*

Auni gathered the little strength he had, expanding his chest, he sang with everything he had left. If he were destined to fail in his quest, he would leave this life and enter the next singing to The One. With his last note still lingering in the air, a large shadow flew over him once, and then again. The last thing he saw, before giving in to exhaustion were claws three times as long as his own and wings that blotted out the heat of the sun.

He felt a breeze drift over and ruffle his feathers. Sighing in relief he inhaled and smelled water. Had he died? Had he failed? He blinked his dry eyes and saw every shade of green leaf sprouting from varying sizes of trees and shrubs, flowers and tall grass. In the center was a pool that reflected the sky so clearly it was like you were looking into the Heavens. He stood up and stretched his aching back, but stumbled in pain when he tried to lift his wings, one had been broken in the fall.

'You need to rest, small one. You are injured and very weak from your journey.' It was a gentle voice that soothed his anxiety.

He glanced around and saw nothing but rocks, but then, one moved and the shadow of a tree shifted closer to him. No not a tree, a neck! He looked up and sat on his tail feathers in awe. She was larger than he had imagined and far more beautiful. Her scales shimmered in the waning sunlight, each one in varying shades of blue, aqua and cerulean. Her eyes held his gaze and looked on him with the wisdom of centuries lived and still they were kind. Her wings were tucked neatly against her side as she reclined near the water, the tip of her tail flicked back and forth not unlike a cat who was at ease in its domain. Her front legs crossed each other and held enormous razor sharp claws. Though she was clearly strong, there was also something gentle about her and it terrified him all the more. It was always the calm ones that could flip and rip you to shreds in a heartbeat. She had two large horns that curved around and faced her back followed by rows of gradually smaller horns that stopped just at the base of her skull, like an ornamental helmet. Each one started as an ice blue and ended tipped in midnight. She was a sight to behold and would strike terror into the hearts of any unfortunate enough to stir her ire.

'I found you! You're real!'

'No, I think I found you! And how could you come all this way if you did not believe I was real?' She said with a smile in her voice, her large oval eyes crinkling in amusement. *'But your song had much to do with that. I was hunting and heard the most beautiful sound, and there you were, floundering in the sand near death. Why are you here? No one ventures into this wasteland without a good reason.'*

'Thank you for your assistance! I am Auni. What should I call you?'

'You may call me, Syphra.'

'Syphra. Yes, I came here to find you actually. The time of the prophecy is at hand and you're needed once more.'

*'I'd hoped you were **not** going to say that. I have slept in this oasis for many years. Only recently I awoke and felt... a kindling in my heart. So, my familiar has been born and with him the new King.'*

'Yes, Syphra. Sadly, it looks as if we must stay here for some time as I cannot travel in my current state. It took me several days to reach you. I can only hope the others are gathering now.'

'Others?'

'Yes, the dire wolves should be gathering as well. Naia, she is our emissary to them, left at the same time I did and I pray she had better luck than I did on her journey.'

'It really has begun then.' She gazed into the distance; her large eyes troubled but she kept her thoughts hidden. *'We must gather one more for this quest to be successful. I will carry you. When we reach the mountains, we can see about healing your wing. We'll leave at nightfall. Eat and replenish yourself at the pool. You will find the results invigorating, for The One has blessed this place.'*

Auni fed until he thought he would burst. He had never tasted fruit so sweet, even the water was sweet. He bathed and as the dust rolled off his feathers, he could not help but sing his thanks to The One for His mercies and blessing. This oasis truly was a balm. He was unable to roost in the tree due to his wing, but found large fronds that had fallen at the base of one tree and bedded down until Syphra was ready to journey back. As night began to fall, he felt a warm breath cross his head. Lifting his beak from the warm spot beneath his wing, he gazed into her large blue eyes..

'Come, it is time to go. Would you be more comfortable in my claw or on my back?'

'I think it would be safer for you, if you carry me in your claw. I would be afraid my own talons and poison might hurt you should I ride on your back.'

Syphra chuckled softly, a rumbling sound deep in her chest. *'Have no fear, my scales are impenetrable by your talons, and even if you could pierce through, I cannot be harmed by your venom. That is why you were chosen to find me. None other could make the journey, but you could defend yourself should any of the desert creatures happen upon you.'* She held out one claw. *'Come, time is short and I am anxious to meet the one who thinks he will ride me into battle.'*

With one beat of her great wings, they lifted into the dark night and circled high above the oasis, giving Auni his first look at it in its entirety. It was a beautiful gem in the middle of the wasteland; he imagined it was even more so in the light of day. He hoped he would be able to return in the future. It would be the perfect nesting ground. Syphra hovered to get her bearings and then tore through the sky toward the north-east, a dark shadow racing across the dunes.

Chapter 17

CHUMBRA STOOD OVER HIS WORK table staring at the ingredients, he was indecisive. He could not remember a time when he was indecisive, but he knew if he mixed this, there would be unfathomable consequences. His work to date had been purely experimental, or for monetary gains. But this, this was different. He had sworn his allegiance to the Dark Lord out of necessity, self-preservation. He would not call himself a *true* believer, not until recently when all he had witnessed left little doubt in his mind that the Dark Lord was, in fact, real. Even so, he was loyal to himself, above all else. He walked away from the table to the window and glanced at the street below. It was void of normal traffic; people had taken to staying indoors as much as possible. There was no laughter from children, no bartering in the marketplace. Business was conducted in hurried whispers and no one dared venture out after dark. The once green and fruitful lands lay barren. King David's paranoia had reached levels even he could not have predicted. He was consumed with ensuring he was always the strongest in the room. He had gone through three captains of the guard since Akronius' defection. Their bodies were strapped to poles at the gates of the manor with a nail driven through the mouth to secure them as a visible sign of what happened to those unfortunate enough to garner the King's ire. David's brutality had no limits, especially with the advisors around him whispering in his ear day and night. There was a time that King David would have balked at innocent bloodshed, but that time had passed. Nothing was off limits. And even Chumbra felt the noose closing in around his throat. He had to remain useful or find a stake of his own. Returning to the table he added the ingredients to a mortar bowl and began pounding with his pestle.

King David sat on his throne. The heavy drapes around him were closed, surrounding him in the darkness he had come to love, he had stopped fighting it, he embraced who he was and looked forward to becoming even more. No one disturbed him, no one dared. He would soon hold all the power in the land. He would attack his enemies with an iron fist, striking like a shadow and disappearing just as quickly. Vicrano was dead but his daughter lived, a puppet to Ashrek. Overton and Alcherist were plotting somewhere in their distant hovels and Akronius's defection proved that he had indeed found the heir and was now a traitor. He had spies of his own and had tracked them down to a small cottage by the river. Yes, they were gifted but untrained. They were children playing adult games. His spy had reported that the boy, his... cousin, grieving a father he never knew, had been guided by Akronius to his crypt. He'd had his men go there to kill them, but somehow, they had been able to evade capture. He would save them for last. He would have Chumbra use the blood of this man-child to create another spell. Surely there was something that would enable him to live forever. If only his mother could see him now, he laughed to himself, she had thought him weak.

"Look at me now, Mother!" He shouted to the empty room. "You thought to mold me into your image, to make me stronger! But *you* were the weak one! Look where all your scheming and manipulation got you, *nowhere*! I sit on the throne you coveted and you are DEAD! DEAD! Ha-ha-ha!" His manic cackling filled the room, bouncing off the walls and echoing down the halls.

Chumbra stopped his mixing and turned to the door. He thought he heard laughter, but that could not be right, there was no happiness in this place. All the servants, save the ones loyal to the Dark Lord, had long ago abandoned their posts. Returning his focus to the task at hand, he added the last ingredient, the blood of King Kaison. Holding his hand above it he uttered the necessary words and watched it bubble in the bowl until only a sticky, tar-like substance remained. He gathered this in a vial and turned for the door.

Exiting his chamber, he bumped directly into a servant.

"Watch where you're going!" He shouted in frustration.

"I'm sorry, My Lord! The King has requested the presence of all servants for an announcement. I would suggest you hurry as well."

Chumbra paused, he had not been summoned. What was going on? Instead of following the servant, he made his way to Lady Devona's old room. He found the hidden doorway and entered the tunnel system. Along the route, he could hear hurried footsteps scurrying quickly on the other side of the stone wall. Reaching the throne room, he peered through the small gap that was between two pillars and hidden deep in the shadows. He saw the king pacing on the Dais, and the few servants left were pushed to the front of the room by guards.

"It has come to my attention that not all of you are as loyal as you claim. Some of you harbor unbelief and doubt my right to be King. You have heard the whispers of another heir and are spreading *lies*!" He shouted, "Still, others have proven their value to me and revealed who the would-be traitor is." He made eye contact with several of the servants, and then glanced up and locked eyes with Chumbra, smiling malevolently. How had he known where to look? Chumbra was shocked, but could not look away from what was unfolding before him.

"I see you little mouse, the shadows cannot hide you from their master, but your time has not yet come. I have caught a far bigger rat for now. Sclera! Where are you?"

A skinny man stepped forward, bony trembling hands clasped together. "Here, Your Majesty."

"It has been said that you wish to see another on the throne. Is this true?"

"No, Your Majesty! I am loyal to the King, I swear it!"

"Yes, you are loyal, but to which king? Have you never spoken an ill word against me? Never spoken of my predecessor in comparison to me? Never *wished* for what you perceive as better days?" King David leaned forward with narrow eyes and spittle in the corner of his mouth. "Never gave information to our enemies?" Each word said with sarcasm, his face twisted in disgust. The man stuttered vainly in his defense, looking around for assistance.

"Guards, bring in our guests!" King David bellowed as a sinister gleam sparked in his eye.

The doors opened once more and a woman was dragged in, a small child at her side and a swaddled baby in her arms. Blood smeared her hands and the lower portion of her face as she mumbled and cried incoherently.

"Oh no, Your Majesty! Please don't hurt my family! I'm begging ya, PLEASE! I'll do anything! SAY anything! Only leave them! Please, oh please." The man fell to his knees as his wife and children were dragged to the front of the room.

"Such a lovely family you have, your son looks like he will grow into a tall, strong man. But will he follow your footsteps or his King?" He grabbed the woman by her curly dark brown hair and yanked her head back, her hazel eyes going wide and her caramel skin blanching in fear. "Your wife is past her prime, but I'm sure I could still find a use for her, even missing her tongue." He locked eyes over her head with Sclera, who was close to his breaking point, openly weeping and still begging for their lives. David could taste the fear in the air and it pleased him immensely.

"But look!" He parted the blanket in the woman's arms to reveal an infant. "Look at what we have here." He gently took the child from the woman's grip as she groaned in protest. He walked away from her and called the boy who looked to be about seven years old. "Come here boy." He stood there with the boy at his side and the baby in his arms and addressed the room.

"What is your name?"

The boy was frozen. David bent toward him, his dark eyes piercing as they demanded an answer.

"Jacob," the boy whispered through teeth that chattered.

David straightened and looked around at all present. "This is what will happen to all who speak or even *think* against me. I will *always* find you. I am more powerful than all of you and soon I will be more powerful than anyone in the entire land. I WILL BE A GOD! Take them!"

His guards rushed forward and took hold of the man and his wife. "You will go to your death knowing I will raise your son in my own image, and your infant daughter will be sacrificed at dusk to honor our Dark Lord." He smiled and seemed to preen in the screams of the man and his wife as they were dragged from the room. "Anyone else have doubts?" He gazed around the room, "No? Good, get back to your duties. Except you, little mouse. Stay right where you are, please."

The room emptied quickly and the King glanced once again at Chumbra's hiding place as he handed the infant to a nearby guard, keeping one hand on Jacob's thin shoulder he crooked a finger. "Come out, come out, little mouse."

The hidden door creaked open slowly, dust falling from unused hinges as Chumbra emerged on shaky legs. "Yes, Your Majesty, how can I be of service?"

King David kept the menacing grin on his face as he watched Chumbra squirm, the silence stretching beyond what was comfortable before shoving the small boy toward him. "Here, take Jacob as your apprentice, teach him all you know. But more importantly, teach him loyalty to me alone. Understand?"

"Yes, Your Majesty." Chumbra bowed respectfully and grabbed the boy's arm.

Jacob was shaking, his entire body shivering in shock and fear. Yet from somewhere he found the courage to speak. "No! I want my mother! Where is my sister? Give me my sister! No, I won't go with you!"

Chumbra saw the King out of the corner of his eye and knew what he did now could impact how long he lived. He gave the boy a slap across the face to silence him, his hand leaving a rapidly developing purple bruise on his caramel complexion.

"Your parents are dead as your sister will be soon. You will obey me, and we serve the King." He could feel the boy deflate beside him and saw the evil smile that lit the King's face. He exited the room, the vial in his pocket all but forgotten.

Chapter 18

LORD OVERTON DISREGARDED THE SECOND letter from his son Ashrek, he cast the unopened missive on the table with a flick of his wrist; he had no time to hand-hold the boy. He would simply have to figure things out on his own until he had his own plans in place. Overton looked over the maps of the completed tunnel and the trade route that circled the mountain by the sea. Now that he had access and control of the roads, he could start taxing the people who traveled it and the funds would be used to build his army. He had set up the west side of Vimeo to accept those fleeing King David's rule in Elhaanai, he was poised to be the benevolent leader the people so desperately wanted right now.

He put the refugees to work clearing debris from the streets and felling trees for spears. Those not talented in the making of weapons were tasked with farming and irrigation. Through Ashrek he had possession of Arcana, but he wanted to expand his boundaries into the desert. There had to be a way to make the land there yield, and if not, he hoped to find something of value buried within its dunes. There were enough legends and hearsay regarding dragons and treasures to back up his searching. And his brother, yet again, opposed him in this venture; claiming the desert to be a waste of resources and that they should seek to take stronger control over Arcana, insisting Ashrek was not up to the task. Ashrek had proven competent so far, there was no reason he would not continue to follow orders. His only task was to gain control and then wait for instruction. He was not strong enough to try and take power for himself, Lord Overton dismissed the thought immediately. Alcherist was a paranoid man, obsessed with revenge when he should be looking for a cure for his bewitched son. Overton shivered at the thought of the child. He had heard the servants gossiping in the halls about the wounds given to his sister-in-law from her attempts to nurse the possessed child. Sybella truly was the Dark Lord's spawn to so hex a baby. But that mattered little to him in the grand scheme of things. He would be king as he had been meant to be and his son would be heir. Alcherist could have other children, they should dispose of that affliction and be done with the whole affair. He shook his head in disgust and called for the captain of his guard.

"Any word from our spy?"

"Reports have come in that the spy placed in King David's manor was discovered and executed yesterday along with his wife."

Overton scrubbed his hands over his face. "And his family?"

"The boy has been placed in the care of Chumbra and the infant… was sacrificed to the Dark Lord at dusk yesterday."

"My god, the man has truly lost his soul!" Lord Overton glanced out the window at the setting sun. He had offered the man escape if he could gather enough information about the state of David's army. It would be difficult to find a replacement now, he was sure this information was already spreading through the streets.

"We'll have to use the information we have for now. It does not appear that their army has been doing any new training drills. He has executed three captains in the time since his favorite defected for this mystery heir. He is waiting on his Oracle Chumbra to prepare something that would give him some power that we know nothing of." Lord Overton sighed in frustration, leaning heavily on both arms, hands, palm down on the massive wooden table before him. "For now, continue to prepare our armies. Put the influx of men from Elhaanai through rigorous drills but do not waste too much time on them, they will be placed at the front when we march on Elhaanai, and save the best armor for our own men."

"As you say, Sir." The captain struck his fist across his chest and left the room.

Overton looked again at the map and smiled, the three provinces had been divided since the battle of Eckter, King Vernis had defeated the uprising and the land fragmented. The people did not want another king, feeling such a ruler did not truly hear their needs from a high throne. And who was he to determine whom they could worship? No, instead lords had been elected, but that would all change soon. They would be free to worship and live as they pleased but the land would be united under one king again, a king whom they would obey and follow, he would be that king.

Lord Alcherist stood in the shadows of an alcove and listened to the whispering in the halls about the murder of his brother's spy. Overton was a fool who thought too highly of his own intelligence. Victory could only come by working together with Arcana against

Elhaanai. True, in the beginning he was against the alliance. But now as things had unfolded he knew they must absorb Arcana into themselves, and extend Vimeo to the sea, not into the desert to die. They would stand the best chance at wiping out all followers of this Dark Lord and his emissary, David. As king, he could show the people the best path forward was one of unity, with no alliance to any higher power. Neither The One nor the Dark Lord brought anything but pain, death and futile hopes. He had never wanted to be king; his dream had been to spend his days with a happy family. A son to carry his name on, and a beautiful wife to spend his days and nights with. Now, thanks to Sybella, his dreams had been distorted. He would have to lower himself to her level to drag his family back from the brink of oblivion.

Ashrek knew his father was ignoring his letters. He had received no response to the last two he had sent. His father thought he was still a boy under his rule, following orders. He had grown too accustomed to the weak-willed character they had created to fool Vicrano. He was not that simpering fool; he was a man and a strong one at that, in control of his own manor, his own soldiers and a very powerful priestess. Both his father and his uncle would come to regret their decision to underestimate him.

Walking down the dimly lit halls toward Sybella's room, he flexed his fists in frustration, he would prove everyone wrong. Sybella had only a few days left until the full moon, she had better be prepared. He did not bother knocking.

"Sybella, good evening. How are the preparations coming?" She was standing before a table covered in leather bound books with strange writing on them. Bowls and vials littered every surface in the room except for the small bed that she slept on. There was a faint smell of decay in the air. Looking around he found the cause; she had kept the hound from her first night. It lay on the same platter, nothing more than a skeleton.

"Do you like it, My Lord?" Sybella asked, seeing where his attention had drifted. "I thought it added a bit of macabre charm to the room. After all, you were so thoughtful to send it to me." Sybella leaned heavily on her cane and hobbled across the room to a chair by the fire. "Please excuse my disrespect by sitting. My leg is still too weak to support me for very long."

Ashrek ran his finger along several books on the table, unable to read their titles and took the seat opposite her. "Think nothing of it. Tell me, how close are you to completing your task?"

Ignoring his question completely, she gazed lovingly at her texts. "The leather holds up well no matter how many times I open and close their pages. Human skin is very adaptable." She stared at Ashrek, and only a small twitch of his fingers displayed his displeasure at having touched something so vile. "I will be ready for you on the night of the full moon. A servant is bringing me a few more ingredients for my fertility and your virility. I will have someone summon you once it is ready. You will be able to test it on a subject of your choosing before taking it yourself."

Ashrek nodded in agreement. "I am glad you are aware of my mistrust. Continue your work. I will send some food for you shortly." He left her there, staring into the flames surrounded with her skin bound books and bones.

<h1 style="text-align:center">Chapter 19</h1>

SYPHRA HELD AUNI CLOSE to her body, this high in the mountains it was very cold and he needed her body heat. As they began their descent, Auni looked around but could see nothing beyond the swirling clouds. Surrounded in a blanket of white, there were no sounds other than the beat of Syphra's large wings and her breathing. Breaking through the clouds, a clearing appeared beneath them, the jade colored grass as vibrant as the oasis they not long left. A strong looking man stood before them, white locks coiled around on the top of his head and a beaming smile on his brown face.

"Syphra! So good to see you again my old friend," Shama called jovially. "The time has come, has it not? And who do you carry with you?"

This is Auni. He is wounded and needs your care. Yes, you are right. The time has indeed come.' Syphra settled her large frame into the grass and wrapped her long tail around her, bringing her head down to Shama's level *'So, have you met **him** yet?'*

"Now Syphra, why would you want me to ruin the surprise of your first meeting? You will get nothing from me!" He tapped her snout gently and looked at the bird standing quietly beside her, observing their banter while one wing hung to the ground. "Come Auni, follow me so we can tend to your wounds."

Auni followed the strange man into the house where a stone basin of water was prepared for him. "Get in please." Auni tried to tell the man he had no need for a bath, but was interrupted with a smile and raised hand, "I am not able to understand you Auni. I can speak to Syphra because she is just as old as I am, and we are connected on a deeper level. You must take this step for your healing to begin." Once again he displayed a wise smile. "Trust me."

Auni glanced at the water and then at the man. The One had not failed nor led him astray yet, he would continue to trust the path he'd been set on. The water rippled as he placed one talon into the stone bath, the steam swirling up and around him as he waded into the middle of the pool. It was unlike anything he had ever felt! He ducked his head beneath the surface and cleaned his beak. The water ran in droplets down his head and neck. With each droplet it was as if the bitterness and loneliness he hadn't even known he harbored fell away. He felt lighter and stronger than ever. Springing from the water with wings spread wide he trilled a single pure note from his heart in thanks, higher and clearer than anything he had sung before. It was as if his soul had been cleansed as well. He was so focused on this emotional feeling that he didn't immediately notice he'd been healed. He floated to the floor and looked at the man in awe.

Shama nodded and extended his arm for Auni to exit the home. "The water is from the blessed pool that I watch over. You've been healed and fortified, for the journey ahead will be difficult. But you will find the reward worth it, if you stay the course. I am Shama. I will journey back with you for a time and then return here to my home. You will find the berries outside to be similar to those in the oasis. Eat your fill while I prepare for the journey."

'Syphra! Look! My wing is healed! Shama... the water... it's amazing!'

'Yes Auni, I knew he would be able to help you. He is important to the outcome of the coming battle, and will accompany us.'

'Yes, he told me this as well. I feel so different, lighter!'

'The waters of this place have been blessed by The One. All who bathe in its flow are changed forever.'

Syphra gazed off in the direction of the sacred pool, *'I have not submerged myself in many years, but now is not my time. Go, refresh yourself, I will rest here until we are ready to leave.'*

Syphra curled her long neck around and tucked it under her wing. In a moment, she looked nothing like a dragon; only a pile of varying sized blue gray stones marked where she lay. *"Amazing"* thought Auni as he walked over to a nearby bush, heavy with ripe berries.

Several hours later, Shama emerged from his hut. There was a glow about his face and a peace in the way he approached Syphra. He sat his pack down and patted the rock before him.

"Time to go, my friend. I tried to pack light this time!" He said with a smile. "I remember how you complained and complained about all the useless items I burdened you down with when we last rode into battle." Seeing how attentive Auni was to his words, he cleared his throat and smoothed one of his white locks back into place. "But that is a story for another time. We should be on our way. I never tire of

71

that first glance between rider and dragon; terror and awe mixed together, sometimes equally, and sometimes not!" He chuckled to himself, craning his head back to admire Syphra as she stretched her wings and came back to her full length. Yawning like a sleepy cat, row after row of sharp teeth were visible. Auni pitied the creatures who would fall by her bite.

Now that Auni's wing was healed, Shama took his place in the grasp of Syphra's claw, his pack in the other. Syphra took off and Auni followed her into the frigid air.

'Stay close to me Auni until we reach a lower altitude. My body heat should be enough to keep you warm until then.'

The trio flew down the mountain, heading for the small cottage that sat beside the river and destiny.

Moving silently through the trees, Naia and her brother led their new pack in the same direction. They had visited several other groups and recruited five more wolves. There were now six males and six females, enough to start the next generation of dire wolves when this was all over.

'Naia!'

'Yes Nguvu.'

'You should address me as Alpha when we are with the pack. I know our ways are new to you, but please try.'

'Yes, Alpha.' She was tempted to roll her eyes, but knew he was right. She had been constantly nipped at during the run here. Her place was at the back of the pack until she earned respect in the hierarchy. It did not matter that she was sister to the alpha, at the end of the day she was a half breed and would have to prove herself.

'Are we nearing the human home?'

'Yes, I can smell the river. We will reach it within the hour.'

They continued the journey and paused just out of range of the cottage, when Nguvu addressed her again.

'I can smell a human. Is he part of your man pack?'

Naia sniffed the air and snarled, *'No, he is not. I can almost taste the evil from his skin. Let me take him down.'*

Nguvu looked down at her and understood the need to do this.

72

'Go ahead, we will wait for you here.'

'No, I need you all with me. We must force him toward the camp, they will want to question him.'

'We will follow your lead.' Nguvu said with a nod.

Naia crept into the brush until she was directly behind the man and then growled, low and loud. The man yelped in fear and raised his hands to the sword at his side when another growl sounded to his left and still another to his right. Realizing he was surrounded he began to back up only to hear another menacing growl directly behind him. Finding himself surrounded there was only one route left open for him to take, anytime he tried to detour from the path he was snapped at.

'Akronius, can you hear me?'

'Naia! You're back! Where did you go?'

'I will tell you all in good time, for now, you need to arm everyone and come out of the cottage. I have a gift for you.'

Akronius picked up his sword and turned for the door. "Naia is back, she wants us all armed and outside. Now!"

"I wonder what's going on." Elainea said, stepping outside as her hands began to pulse with blue and white flames. She stood beside Alric who now carried the bejeweled blade. On the other side stood Kaison, armed with two small blades.

"Whatever it is we will meet it head on," Akronius said calmly.

They looked to the edge of the forest and heard growls getting closer. It was still early in the day, but they could see a man being herded their way.

'We found this man spying on the camp.'

"She said they found this man spying on us." Akronius said as he put his sword away and roughly grabbed the man by the arm, twisting it behind his back. "Who sent you?"

"I do not have to tell you anything, traitor! Call off your dogs!" The attempt at bravado was noted but failed miserably as his voice cracked like dry leaves in the wind and sweat dripped down onto his pale face.

"Last chance, who sent you? These *wolves* look hungry to me." Akronius pushed the man closer to the ring of wolves. "I know you are familiar with how sharp the teeth of dire wolves are. They have every reason to hate our kind and I am sure they would be more than happy to tear you limb from limb." Naia snapped her teeth and ran her tongue across them, saliva dripping from her mouth. The man's legs trembled and he almost collapsed in fear.

"Alright! King David sent me weeks ago. I have been reporting back to him periodically. I told him you went to the crypt and was shocked to see you come back, with a new man no less. He will be looking for me, but I can tell him you left, that you all gave up on this delusional quest for the throne and went south. He will believe me, I swear it." The man's eyes were wide with fear. He would say anything to spare his life, no matter how futile he must know it to be.

Akronius shoved the man to his knees so he was face to face with Naia as she stood guard, as he and the others gathered off to the side. "What should we do with him? Obviously, we cannot release him. The wolves could dispatch him, but I would rather they not get a taste for human flesh." He said with a shudder. He knew that he or Kaison could kill the man with little thought. They were used to warfare but the other two were not and that needed to change.

"Alric…?"

But Alric looked down, he could not or would not do it, Akronius turned to Elainea.

"Elainea?" She turned and looked at Alric with pity. Shaking her head she turned to the spy and lifted her blazing hands. A gust of air blew her back and a searing heat skimmed across her face. When she looked up, the spot where the man knelt was filled instead with a steaming pile of… of something that did not resemble a man at all. Looking up in fear, a giant shadow hovered over them. The growls of the wolves silenced immediately and they retreated to a wide circle some distance away. Akronius, Alric and Kaison shielded their eyes as they were buffeted by the wind from the great wings descending from above.

Akronius clutched his chest and fell to one knee with a gasp, feeling something click into place inside him.

Gazing up into large blue eyes his jaw dropped.

'Hello, Akronius.'

<h1 style="text-align:center">Chapter 20</h1>

NO ONE SPOKE FOR A MOMENT as the dragon landed, settled into a comfortable position and released the pack she had been carrying. Auni landed on the nearby fence post and silently watched everything unfold.

"So nice to see everyone again!" Shama said with his signature smile as he came into view. "Akronius, everyone else, this is Syphra. She is…"

"Beautiful." Akronius interrupted him.

'And you are wise.' Syphra replied, sounding pleased.

"Awe, it is then!" Shama chuckled. "Yes, well. We have quite a bit to speak about," he said, gathering his pack and heading for the cottage door. "Good to see you again Kaison! Alric, I can tell you're eating too much. Elainea, we did not mean to steal the fire from you." He chuckled at his own joke. "Syphra wanted to test her death spray and he provided the perfect opportunity."

"Death spray?" Akronius stood, still staring in awe at Syphra, "I thought dragons sprayed fire…"

'We will have the time to get acquainted, now you must listen to what Shama has to say.' Syphra said, bending her head closer to Akronius. He slowly reached out to touch her forehead and it was as if his arm locked onto her. Searing heat coursed through him followed by freezing cold, finally the feeling settled somewhere in the middle and he was released from whatever spell had trapped him.

'We are bonded.' Syphra said with a sigh. *'It has been ages since I have felt that part of me ignited. I have missed it.'*

She relaxed in the grass and watched Akronius open his eyes in wonder.

"It's amazing! *You're* amazing!" Akronius looked around and saw everything as if he had been blind before now. Colors were brighter, he could see clear across the river and into the woods. He could smell everything! It seemed all his senses had heightened and were now in tune with hers. Turning back to her, he was speechless. Syphra nodded and gestured with her large head for him to go inside. They would have time together after Shama spoke to them all.

"Your eyes…" Alric said looking closely at Akronius as he entered the home.

"What about them?" Akronius asked, touching his own face.

"Yes, yes. They have a blue ring around them now. You are bonded to Syphra and have taken on some of her attributes." Shama said absentmindedly. "That is to be expected. Now on to more important matters, well, more *pressing* matters anyway."

Akronius settled, leaning against one of the walls as the table could only seat four. Naia walked into the room with a large wolf just behind her and stood at Akronius' side.

'This is Nguvu, he is the leader of my pack and…my brother.'

Akronius repeated what she said and looked at the larger male with fascination, he spoke out loud for the benefit of those present. "Hello Nguvu, I am Akronius, that is Alric, Elainea, Shama and…"

'Kaison, yes we know who he is.' Nguvu greeted Kaison with a slight lowering of his head, *'I am glad to meet here with you all. I am sorry we could not gather more wolves for the battle, but you understand, we hold no love for mankind.'*

"Every bit of help will be needed in the days to come, thank them for us." Akronius said and then turned to face Shama. "So, what now?"

Shama sat silently, arms raised to his side with palms facing upward, his head was bowed and his lips moved rapidly. The air in the small room became heavy and charged with a force unknown to them. Akronius' fingers twitched toward the sword at his side until Naia whispered to him, *'NO. Be still. Wait. Watch.'* Shama lifted his head revealing eyes that had turned white. He exhaled and the room filled with a fragrance sweeter than any flower could possibly be. Elainea felt her breath quicken and she could not help but lower her face and palms flat on the table under the overwhelming pressure building around her. And though Akronius tried to fight whatever it was that swirled around him, he too found himself lowering into a kneeling position on the floor, his head bowed in submission. Kaison threw his head back and felt tears streaming down his face. Alric sat in silence, arms wrapped around his body and rocked back and forth. The weight of it settled on all of them, it was warm and comforting and terrifying.

"Be at peace my warriors. I have chosen you for this time. Evil entered this

land many years ago and almost destroyed it. One man stood against the tide and thwarted the plans of the Dark Lord. But he is once again trying to gain a foothold and you must stand against it. You have been chosen for your bravery, your loyalty, your wisdom, your cunning and your love. Within each of you lies more vitality and power than you are aware of. Trust yourselves and each other. No man or woman is strong enough to defeat the darkness on their own. DO NOT underestimate it or you will be lost. Although everything lost can be found, it will not be without cost. Time is short, the way is set. You have been courageous to this point, stay the course."

The wind blew in through the open door and the scent slowly lifted from the room, everyone sat in awe of what they had just been part of.

"Amazing and humbling isn't it?" Shama spoke silently, face tilted up and eyes closed with his hands folded across his middle. He sat as if savoring the aftermath of what could only be described as a visitation.

"Was that... did we... did HE..." Elainea could not even complete her sentence. She ran her hands up and down her arms to sooth the goosebumps that had risen there.

"Yes, The One has spoken, giving both blessing and direction." Shama looked around at the small band. "Time to get to work."

Chapter 21

SYBELLA GLANCED OUT OF THE small window at the full moon, she had sent word to Ashrek several hours earlier that she was ready. The fact that he kept her waiting only added insult to her lack of control over the situation, increasing the number of reasons to hate him. She went over what she had to do. She had given Ashrek two vials the day before; one to test and one to use. Of course he had every reason to be wary. Still, she had alternatives, holding her hand before her to admire the unassuming ring that was really a weapon. It was a simple black band with scroll work and leaves weaving around the center; unless you ran your finger across it you would think it was completely smooth. But there was a very sharp point on one of the ivy leaves that wouldn't even leave a mark, but the effects however would be most gratifying. When he came to lie with her, she would only have to scratch him with it and thanks to the poison she had coated it with, his strength would disappear, slowly, over the following days. She looked at the black band and smiled. Revenge would be sweet, slow revenge even sweeter. His strength would leak out of him and as long as she wore the ring, she would soak it up. No one would be able to stop it.

Her door creaked open and she stiffened at the heavy footsteps approaching her.

"Good evening, Wife." Ashrek did not wait for her response as he pushed her onto the bed, roughly.

"Wait! We can't just... STOP! You have to take the potion first." Sybella scrambled from under him and back into the corner of her bed. "You've already tested it, so drink it and be done."

Her voice trembled. She had not expected to be afraid when it came time to fulfill her end of the agreement. Ashrek smiled and stepped away from her. Reaching into his waistcoat, he removed and lifted the vial in a mock salute to her. His face twisted at the bitter taste while his hands moved to the top of his britches. He paused and shook his head a few times, and then looked up. His eyes took on a red tint and she knew the potion was working through his system. She clutched the sheet in fear.

"I know this is your first time Wife, and normally it would be a pleasing experience for both involved, but you will not enjoy this. I will ensure it."

Sybella's breathing quickened and her mouth went dry. It was too late for her to back out now. He did not drain her with his gift so he must have wanted her to fight him. Instead, she removed her nightgown and lay down, turning her face to the wall.

"What is this? Giving in so easily? I think not." He grabbed her arm and dragged her to the floor. He slapped her across the face once and then again on the opposite side. "Look at you! They said you are the most powerful priestess of the Dark Lord. HA! Lies, you are nothing." He shook her roughly. "You are less than nothing and no one will remember you when I am finished with you." He threw her to the floor and kicked her once. "Nothing to say? So be it." He lifted her into his arms and moved her roughly to the bed, so enraged, that he did not notice her hand flop across his neck, nor did he feel the small scratch from her ring. She smiled once more through the throbbing of her bruises and once again faced the wall as she let him have his way. He was a fool. She was strong, and would be far stronger than him soon.

Ashrek groaned as the light hit his eyelids. Shielding them and rubbing his hands over his face, he sat up. Where was he? Looking around the barren room, he remembered. Beside him lay his wife. Her eyes locked with his as he turned toward her, the contempt was clear, along with something smug he could not quite understand.

"How long will it be before we know if this was successful?" he asked, pulling his shirt over his head.

"It was successful." Sybella said confidently, "You will have a son in nine months. Will you place me back in my cell or can I stay here?"

"You will stay in this room. The guard will remain at your door and meals will be brought to you. Your spell books will be removed and burned along with any other evil relics you have here. A cleansing has begun in Arcana, and you are not exempt from it." Ashrek stood and opened the door. He instructed the waiting servants to start clearing the room of all books, vials, and tokens. Ashrek stood and watched Sybella as she sat immobile on the bed, only her eyes moved back and forth as she followed the items one by one as they left her room.

"I will make sure your blood flow is optimal for a strong birth." Ashrek said flatly, gazing at her with indifference, "You will have to give up that ring as well. Nothing is to be left behind."

"Please Ashrek, it is the last thing my father gave me. Please do not remove this one small comfort from me. I beg you!" Sybella managed to force a few tears to her eyes in petition,

"Very well. And food will be brought to you shortly." He closed the door behind him, leaving Sybella with two chairs, an empty table and her bed. Even the compartments she had thought secret had been discovered and emptied. She got up and washed using the bowl a girl had left for her. Dressing, she stood before the window and placed her hand on her belly. Patience, she could almost hear her father's voice, patience.

Lord Alcherist approached the door to his brother's study and paused, in his hand was a letter from King David. Supposedly it was a request asking to meet with them to discuss peace. He knew Lord Overton did not want peace, he wanted power; but perhaps he could be persuaded.

"Enter!" Lord Overton boomed as he heard a knock at the door. Looking up, he dismissed Alcherist the moment he stepped over the threshold. "We are busy, Brother. I have no time to fight over your need for revenge again. You can have more children, let it go."

"No, Brother. That is not why I am here this time. Though I still…" A glance from Overton made him stop. "I have received a letter from King David requesting our presence for peace talks. I think we should consider it." Alcherist held the letter up for all to see, Overton was meeting with his generals and several servants were placing trays of food and drink on the table.

"Let me see this letter." Overton broke the seal and skimmed it before he tossed it aside. "He is a young fool. I will not entertain him and neither should you. We will be marching on Elhaanai within the month, and I will be King as soon as I remove his head from the crown."

"Overton, consider the cost!" Alcherist watched the letter flutter to the floor as his brother lifted a goblet of wine to his lips. "Think of the lives that will be lost. Wouldn't it be better to try to talk to him first? He may yet be reasoned with."

"I do not expect you to understand matters of war Alcherist," Overton said as he placed the now empty cup back down. "You are not made for this. Go home and tend to your sick family. I will call you if I need a pat on the back." Overton laughed at his own insult. His laughter turned into a cough and the cough into choking.

"Are you alright Brother? Someone get him some water!" Alcherist stepped closer to his brother who was gasping for breath. Overton grasped desperately onto Alcherist who assisted him into a chair, his eyes growing wider with each panicked moment.

"Bring a healer. Quickly!" Alcherist ordered the servant who was standing nearby. As the man ran from the room, he leaned closer to his brother's ear and whispered, "well, let's get this over with then." He looked down at his brother whose face was turning a strange purple color. Overton's back was to the generals who were still in the room. Alcherist smiled as realization dawned in his brother's fading eyes, darting a look at the letter and then back at him. Struggling to speak, foam formed at the corners of his mouth as the healer rushed in and pushed Alcherist aside, but it was too late. Lord Overton was dead.

"What happened? Tell me, what happened?" the healer asked, looking at the servants.

"The master... he was here talking to his brother and suddenly he just started to choke! He hadn't eaten anything since breakfast. There is only a small bit of wine left in his cup there on the table." The servant answered in a trembling voice, the others in the room murmuring in agreement.

"Lord Alcherist, I'm so sorry about your brother. Is there anything else you noticed? I know you grieve, but please any detail, no matter how small, could point out what caused his death."

Alcherist wept into his hands that covered his face for a moment before appearing to collect himself, then placed a cloth over his brother's grotesque face. He looked around the room in deep thought. "The Letter!" he shouted. "He was reading a letter from King David just as he began to cough!" He walked over to where it had landed on the floor and made it look like he was going to pick it up.

"NO! Don't touch it. I suspect it contains some poison. That vile King must be dealt with. I will take it with me and inspect it at length."

"No," Alcherist said sharply, "you should not touch it either. Is there a way you can inspect it here?"

"Well, I suppose so, if you have no need for it?" Alcherist shook his head. "I could simply toss it in the fire. If there is poison on it, the flame will change color."

"Do it." Alcherist ordered.

Using the edge of his cloak, the healer lifted the parchment and tossed it into the fire. As the seal melted away, the fire turned a bright green. "Poison! King David poisoned Lord Overton!" As the flames destroyed the letter, the healer never noticed the handwriting on it, nor how it favored Lord Alcherist's own hand.

Chapter 22

AKRONIUS WALKED OUTSIDE THE SMALL home and turned his face up toward the sun, the warmth reminded him of the recent experience with The One.

'Amazing isn't it? That one so high could look so low and see us,' Syphra said with a tilt of her head.

"Yes, it is." Akronius agreed, taking a deep breath. "Shama says we should start working together. Get better acquainted."

'That is true. Come, we should be a distance away from the others in case anything goes wrong.'

"Wrong? Wrong how?"

'You need to learn to ride me. If you want the others to witness your failed attempts that's fine with me.' Syphra appeared to shrug one of her large shoulders as she walked toward the river.

"Oh, no. You're right, let's keep my public humiliation to a minimum." Akronius followed Syphra to begin their training. Kaison watched them with a bit of envy evident across his face.

'Are you alright?'

"Yes, I am fine…" Kaison whipped his head to the side to where Naia sat watching him. "I heard you!" The moment he realized this he was filled with a rush of warmth that he remembered very well.

'Yes, you did.' Naia said, she was glad his gift had returned. The sadness she sensed in him would lessen now, and more so when he found a new bond mate.

Kaison knelt before the wolf, he buried his fingers in her fur, laughing and bowed his head until their foreheads touched. Instantly, there was a familiar burning in his blood. Unlike his bond with Shierra, which felt like wind rushing through his veins, this was warm like the sun on fresh soil. It was grounding and deep. He opened his eyes and felt his senses sharpen. Standing, he whispered thanks to The One for this mercy. He'd been floundering, now he stood on firmer ground.

"And it would seem you are my new bond mate Naia." Calling on the training of his youth, he focused on Naia and her heartbeat until his was synchronized, and then together they howled.

Shama smiled from within the home, those two would do well together. He was more concerned with Alric and Elainea. Even now, Alric was complaining about being hungry, and Elainea was rushing about trying to find something to cook.

"ALRIC!" It was as if thunder had clapped in the room. "Shut your mouth! Elainea, sit down!" They both rushed to obey. Shama took a deep, calming breath. "Now, you cannot rely on the strength and wisdom of Akronius and your father. You must be strong in your own right, strong beyond the natural gifts you possess. The One has given special instructions concerning the two of you. It will be painful, but it is necessary."

The two youths nodded but remained silent. "It has been almost a year since your full gifts manifested. Much has happened to you in that time, but there is still much to come. Elainea, you will start your training with me first. Alric, I want you to meditate, see if you can enter a calm enough state to have a vision. You will need that focus and peace in weeks coming."

Shama stood and beckoned Elainea to follow him. In his peripheral view he could see the scowl on Alric's face. It was as he feared, using the second sight, he saw the void flare wider and then disappear beneath the blue and white swirls of Alric's gifts. He sent a silent plea to The One for more time.

Standing in the clearing, Shama instructed Elainea, "Connect to your brother and use his ability to create a shield around us that extends about 300 mitras in all directions. What we are about to do must be contained."

Elainea didn't need to close her eyes anymore to find the blue thread connecting her to Alric, only focus on its familiarity. Normally it was very easy to pull on the connection but this time it was as if there was something holding it back. She had to work very hard to pull enough to create a shield around them.

"That was unusually hard, Shama." She huffed.

"Tell me what it felt like and looked like," Shama answered.

"It was as if the link was stuck in mud. Dark mud. What does that mean?"

"It could be nothing." Shama cast a quick glance back at the home before returning his attention to the young woman beside him. "Or it could be something. Right now, focus on your training. You have primarily relied on your flame to attack and your voice to shriek at your brother. Now you will learn to use fire as a defense and we will work on attacking with your voice. We know you are able to project sound, you need to work on directing it more accurately as a weapon." Shama moved to stand behind her. "Do you see the sapling over there on the edge of the property? Aim your voice at it."

Elainea faced the tree and yelled as loud as she could at the tree, it splintered violently.

"Very good, now you must practice finesse. You know how to whistle, correct?" Elainea nodded, "Whistle at the stone there."

Elainea did as she was asked and missed the stone entirely, but created quite a gouge in the earth.

"Now you know what you must practice. This can be used from great distances and cause immense damage. Sound is created in a clap, a stomp, or a laugh. Once you are able to master every sound your body creates, you will be able to master the sounds of others and in turn use them as a weapon or defense. Use your connection with Alric to see the sound and thereby better direct it."

With that he started to walk away.

"I thought you said this would be painful?"

"I did, but I did not say which one of you would be in pain."

<h1 style="text-align:center">Chapter 23</h1>

ALRIC SAT AT THE TABLE and attempted to focus like Shama had instructed. It was just so quiet. His stomach rumbled loudly in the silence. How could he focus when he was hungry? His eyes roved over the table and lit with inspiration, a light snack would help and then he could get to business.

Shama walked in to find Alric with a large slab of ham between two slices of bread on its way to his face, eyes filled with happiness and then embarrassment.

"Umm I was hungry. I was going to start meditating right after I've finished this."

"I'll wait." Shama sat across from Alric. Unblinking, he watched him take the first bite and then a second.

"Actually, I'm fine. I'll save this for later. We should get started." Ashamed, Alric placed the plate off to the side and waited for Shama to direct him.

"Soooo… what should I do?" Alric asked as he fidgeted in his seat

"You tell me," Shama said, keeping his second sight on the void that was flaring with more consistency. "You need to be able to place yourself in a state where you can have a vision. You need to focus on The One and then wait for Him to speak. The more you do this, the easier it will be to hear His voice."

"Or, I could hold the sword and see if it happens again." Alric jumped up excitedly and went to get his sword. Placing it on the table, his enthusiasm deflated seeing Shama's eyes widen.

"Where did you get this?" Shama locked eyes with Alric.

"Akronius gave it to me, but he got it from my... from Wleia. We know it belonged to a great soldier long ago."

"This sword is cursed." Shama stood and circled the table to stand next to Alric. "It was hidden for a long time for good reason. How it found its way to you, only the Dark Lord knows. You say you had a vision when you held it?"

"Yes."

"Tell me what you saw."

"There was a man standing on top of a hill in full armor. I couldn't see his face. He was surrounded by soldiers and around those soldiers were two banners circling in opposite directions. Over the banners a face was visible at times. A loud cry sounded from the distance and the man yelled for attack, pointing at the nearest banner; the red one with black lightning streaks through it."

"The banners represent Arcana, red with black lightning, and the green with gold is Vimeo. In the vision, the person on the hill was most likely the King of Elhaanai. The face would be the Dark Lord." Shama's shoulders drooped. He had even less time than he thought if this vision was to be believed.

"So, are we supposed to attack Arcana and not King David? Or is King David going to attack Arcana?" Alric said with a furrowed brow.

"I am not sure. I must inquire of The One for guidance." Shama turned and headed toward the bedroom that had once belonged to Wleia.

"What about my training?" Alric asked.

"See if Akronius can instruct you with the sword. But do not touch the gem on the hilt! Its powers are far stronger and more dangerous than simple manipulation of time, you cannot control it." Shama held Alric's gaze with his own.

"All I hear is how I am destined to be king. How my defensive abilities are just as important as offensive ones and yet *no one* is taking the time to train me in them. I finally get a strong weapon and am told I am too *weak* to wield it. My gifts are useless and I'm tired of being passed over! I want to be trained properly!" Alric's harsh words revealed his bitterness.

"I understand Alric, trust me. Your gifts are not useless and you're not being passed over. The One has His hand on you, you need to be patient. Trust Him, Obey Him…." Shama tried to calm Alric down. He could see the dark void flaring rapidly just beneath the boy's surface.

"NO! You don't understand!" Alric's yelling had brought the others to the doorway in concern. Pushing past them into the cold yard he continued, "*None* of you understands. Akronius is literally a murderous, vengeful man. My father was dead and lost his gift only to get it back and bond with a *dire wolf*!" Alric scoffed and sunk his fists into his hair in frustration. "And Elainea, my dear, dear sister is a natural warrior who has no problem killing spies while I cower in shame!" Alric's face took on a mottled look as his tirade reached its pinnacle. "WHY am I even HERE?"

As he screamed these last words, a dark light shot out from him in a wide circle, hitting everyone around him and throwing them back several feet. He swayed once and then collapsed. A few moments later Akronius came to with a groan. Looking around, he saw Shama kneeling over Alric's still form.

"What was that?" He asked quietly. The others were slowly rousing from the ground around them.

"That was an Agiza. In essence, it was the darkness within being used as a weapon against those without. When the twins first came to me, I noticed a streak of darkness in their auras. We all have a bit of darkness within us, and only we can decide to feed it or not. I had no idea if it would ever manifest or if it would be stifled, extinguished. Elainea has successfully rid herself of this darkness, but Alric..." Shama sighed sadly. "He has displayed disappointment over his gifts in the past. It seems he let that bitterness take root and fester. The sword you gave him has a gem in its hilt that slows time. But it also deepens the darkness within. What would take someone years to harbor and gripe over before exploding, takes only moments in the time lapse. In reality, he may only be minimally bothered by his seemingly useless gifts, but the gem will magnify those feelings until he explodes. If used often enough, those explosions can kill him and all those around him."

"Can it be controlled?" Akronius looked down at Alric's pale face.

"Not without killing the wielder."

"Can it be destroyed?"

"Only in the fires that forged it, at the temple of the Dark Lord in Arcana." Shama said sadly.

Chapter 24

SEVERAL HOURS LATER, Alric still had not awakened. Akronius had moved him to the bedroom. His sister sat vigil beside him.

"Why hasn't he awoken yet, Shama?" Kaison asked with concern.

Shama sat in the corner of the room, legs folded and hands clasped in meditation. He stood up and approached the bed. He placed one hand slightly above Alric's head and the other over his chest, he could feel the heat radiating from the boy's body.

"He is in a trance-like state. See how rapidly his eyes move though they are closed? He is seeing something though I don't know what. I have seen this only once before, and I was just as helpless then as I am now."

"Who was it?" Elainea asked with a trembling voice, clutching his limp hand in hers.

"The original owner of that sword." Shama said, gesturing to the other room where it still lay on the table. "He was very strong. He had honed the ability of the Agiza to target only those he chose, but he used it too often and for too long. When he came to me, he was near death."

Shama reached for the bowl on the nearby stool and wrung out a cloth, placing it on Alric's forehead. "He collapsed and ended up in the same state as our friend here. We, Oracles, call it the crucible. It is a state used by The One on those who have great potential, but either can't or won't allow Him to use them."

"What happens in this crucible?" Akronius asked. "Do you know of any who have recovered from it?"

"History tells both sides. Some recovered and told of conversations with an unseen force. Others recounted trials and battles they fought, and some report nothing." Shama leaned against the wall and looked each person in the eye, letting his silence hang in the air. "He'll be refined or he'll die. We must be prepared for either outcome."

"What happened to King Vernis?" Elainea asked. A tear escaped her eye as his silence, once again, was her only answer.

Alric looked around and could see only darkness, he had no idea where he was or what had happened. The last thing he remembered was a searing pain ripping his insides apart. He tried to feel around him but couldn't see his hands, did he even have hands? A body? Panic began building inside him and he couldn't breathe. He felt the weight of the dark nothingness closing in on him! Feeling like he was spinning out of control he tried to scream for help but no sound came out. HELP! He screamed internally as he felt his consciousness begin to float away, he was nothing. No one would help him.

"Alric, why do you doubt my gifts?"

Alric looked around again, and finally saw a faint glow in the distance. "What? Who's there? Can you help me?"

"Why do you doubt that I know what is best for you?"

"Who…. I don't doubt you."

"Why don't you trust the gifts I gave you?"

Alric could feel something building around him, at the same time an intense pressure began to squeeze him from all sides. He tried to push against it but he wasn't strong enough.

"I don't doubt the gifts. They are very good. I trust you." He said rapidly, the pressure squeezing him closer. He was in a cage! He extended his arms into the darkness, feeling the bars, they were warm beneath his fingers and the longer he held onto them, the hotter they became.

"Alric, why do you doubt my gifts?"

"I DON'T! I SWEAR IT! PLEASE STOP! HELP ME!" Alric couldn't move, the bars pressed on him with even the slightest movement, now so hot that he was burned wherever it came in contact with his body.

"Alric, do you know who I am?"

"YES!" Alric was almost crying now, the pain penetrating deep inside him. He trembled under its weight.

"Alric, who are you?"

"I am the son of King Kaison and Queen Alanna. Heir to the throne of… of… Elhaanai." Alric could barely speak but felt the bars widen away from him with that truth.

"Alric, why do you doubt me?"

"I don't. I… aaaahhhh!" The bars quickly returned to their previous position burning him. Truth, he had to speak the truth. He sobbed with the

knowledge. "I doubt! ALRIGHT! I doubt you! I doubt you…" he felt the tears tracking down his face, his body shaking from the release of letting that weight go.

"Why?"

"My gifts are weak!" He spat in anger and frustration as the bars shifted further from him with each honest word. "How can I be King when I'm weak? My sister is stronger than me! EVERYONE is stronger than me! I don't deserve to be King. I do not WANT to be King. I'm not worthy." Alric sank to the floor of his prison as the light drew closer.

"You are not weak Alric. I have been protecting you from the moment you were conceived. I knew you before you were, I know you now and I know who you are meant to become. Will you trust me?"

"I want to… but… how? I'm afraid I'll let you down. Let everyone down." Alric remained on his knees, head bowed to his chest.

"Do you believe in me? My plan for you?"

"I want to," Alric whispered. "Help me believe."

"I will."

Alric gasped as a fire more intense than anything he'd ever witnessed, stronger and hotter than anything his sister had ever conjured, engulfed him. He could feel it inside him and all around him, he was going to die.

"So be it." Alric surrendered to the pain.

"Ahhhhh!" Alric gasped, squeezing the hand that held his own until its owner screamed in pain, and everything faded to black once again.

Chapter 25

ALCHERIST STOOD BEFORE A ROOM of advisors and citizens, his brother's body laid out on a dais before him.

"Today is a sad day, as we lay my brother, Lord Overton to rest. He was taken from us by a cruel and evil man. He was taken before his time." Murmurs began to spread throughout the room as people agreed with him. "He was MURDERED! And for what? For giving those fleeing from this evil man, a safe place to call home. For *daring* to look this usurper in the face and say you are wrong!" Lord Alcherist looked around the room, meeting several gazes and seeing the emotions his words created move like ripples through the crowd. "He was killed for valuing all lives, not just the natural born citizens of Vimeo, but everyone who would look for a better and safer future for their families. We will not let this crime go unpunished. David is no 'king' to us! I will carry on my brother's work and together we will avenge ALL those who have died by his hand. Are you with me?" He shouted passionately.

"KING ALCHERIST! KING ALCHERIST! KING ALCHERIST!" the people shouted. The walls shook from the stomping of many feet, as the swords clanged against the shields of his soldiers, echoing throughout the manor.

A funeral pyre was erected just outside of the city walls and the people swarmed en masse to bid a final goodbye to their beloved Lord Overton. He'd called a three-day period of mourning for refugees and citizens alike, allowing the labor on the desert side of the city to be temporarily forgotten. Alcherist graciously observed it all in silence, knowing his time had come. As the fire was lit and the first ashes drifted up into the evening sky, he turned toward the captain of the guard,

"Prepare a contingent of men. We'll ride to Arcana to inform my nephew of his father's death."

"Yes, My Lord." the captain said, thumping his fist to his chest in salute.

Alcherist headed to his wife's chambers. Today was a better day for her. Elmeera sat in front of the window instead of lying in bed, still with her eyes open, but unseeing.

"My love, I am sorry you could not attend the funeral of my brother. It was truly a sight to behold." He watched her face for any signs that she had heard him, but none came. "I'll be traveling to Arcana to see Ashrek. I must inform him of his father's death. I will return as soon as I'm able." Placing a kiss on her forehead, he headed to the adjoining room to see his son. The child was growing at an alarming rate. He was restrained within a crib made from iron, and even the bars bore the scars from his sharp teeth. The child gnawed on a wooden toy and silently watched his father enter the room.

"Khal, I am sorry to keep you like this. I would love nothing more than to hold you in my arms again, to play with you and teach you like any other child. I *promise* I will heal you. I love you my son." Alcherist knelt just out of reach of the bars. The child had scratched him the last time he ventured too close. Khal's eyes switched from black to green to black again, gnashing his teeth against the bars and hissing at his father.

"Da'da!" Khal said cheerily, causing Alcherist to look up in shock. The boy's eyes were as green as grass in the spring. He rushed forward reaching for the child.

"Yes Khal! Yes! Da'da is here!" Tears leaked down Alcherist's face as he stroked the child's curly haired head. "You remember Da'da? You… AAARRRGGGHHH!" Khal's eyes flipped to black as he sunk his teeth into the flesh of Alcherist's forearm. Ripping his arm from the bars, he clutched it to his chest. The child sat in the corner laughing with glee at the pain he had caused, blood dripping down his chin.

"You'll not always be like this Khal, I promise you!" Alcherist left the room with the sound of his child's manic laughter floating behind him.

"Da'da! Da'da!"

A knock sounded at the door of Alcherist's chambers as he finished bandaging his wound. "The men are ready My Lord." With only a passing glance at his arm, the captain of the guard stepped to the side, following as Alcherist exited the manor.

"Very good, I will be riding hard. Make sure the men keep up." Alcherist said grimly as he mounted his stallion. It stamped its large black hooves and tossed its head as if sensing his rider's anxiety. It was a beautiful animal which had belonged to his brother once, and now it was his, as was everything else. Flicking the reins, the animal bolted forward and the others fell in line. They raced through the gates toward the main road. Citizens could jump out of the way or be trampled.

Sybella stood at the small window in her room watching the setting sun. Ashrek had been true to his word and kept her well-fed. She was strong and though crooked; her leg had healed. Ashrek would be visiting her today, as he had done every day since the conception, to hear the child's heartbeat. He appeared to have a softer side that became clearer each time he heard the gentle beating, but she wouldn't be fooled into believing he would keep her alive after the birth. She was still a prisoner and he was still a murderer.

On the horizon a cloud of dust grew, riders from the west. She watched with interest as they thundered through the gates. Her eyes widened as she saw it was Lord Alcherist. What could he possibly want? She moved to the chair and waited for Ashrek to arrive, wondering which way the tides would turn next.

Chapter 26

UNCLE! WHAT BRINGS YOU TO the dark side?" Ashrek said, as he embraced Alcherist, who noticeably stiffened in response. "I'm only joking! I know you're the last person who would want to be in this vile place. I can only imagine how my father coerced you into coming in his stead."

Ashrek gestured for his uncle to have a seat, as several servants brought in platters of food and wine.

"Nephew, it is good to see you as well. And yes, your father did send me, but not in the way you think." Alcherist paused and sickly-sweetly softened his voice, "Ashrek, I couldn't let another bring you the news I sadly bear. Your father was killed, Ashrek. He was poisoned."

The glass in Ashrek's hand that he was raising to his lips stilled. His knuckles turned white from gripping it so hard. Slowly he lowered his hand, revealing eyes that had turned from their normal slate to granite.

"Who did this?" his voice as hard as his eyes.

"Several days ago, we received a letter from King David requesting an audience to discuss peace. It was addressed to your father so I did not open it myself, though now I wish I had. We believe, and later found it to be true, that a poison had been mixed with the wax seal. When your father broke that seal, the poison came in contact with his skin and entered his body. He died quickly, and when we threw the letter in the fire, the changing color of the flame proved this theory true." Alcherist reached across the table and grasped the forearm of his nephew. "King David murdered your father. We had the ceremonial pyre and burial and I rushed straight here to tell you."

"Uncle, I need a moment. Please excuse me. You," he gestured to a nearby servant, "show my uncle to a suitable room where he can rest."

"Of course, Ashrek. I understand. Call for me when you're ready to discuss the next steps." Lord Alcherist inclined his head as his nephew quickly exited the room. The boy had always been emotional; he'd have to prod him in the right direction if his plan was going to work.

Following the servant down a dimly lit hall Alcherist asked, "What's your name, young man?"

"Marcell, M'lord." The boy replied.

"Marcell, thank you for your assistance. I'm afraid my nephew is greatly distressed at the passing of his father, as am I."

"Yes, M'lord. It's a very sad thing to hear."

"Hopefully his wife will be a comfort to him during this time. Is she well? I didn't see her when we arrived." Alcherist knew the servants would have the most accurate information and be more forthcoming than his nephew when asked.

"Well... yes M'lord she is alright. I suppose." Marcell hesitantly answered, looking uncomfortable with the line of questioning.

"No need to be worried, Marcell. I'm only looking out for the welfare of my family. Ashrek will have to take on his father's responsibilities in Vimeo. I'm sure he'll need trustworthy men to remain here and take care of running the manor. You seem just the sort of man for that job. I can tell you take your duties very seriously." Alcherist could see the boy stand just a bit more erect with his words of praise.

"Thank you, M'lord! This is your room for the night. I will call you when Lord Ashrek is available. Lady Sybella is indeed well, Sir. She is with child and keeps to her quarters. I bring her meals and will tell her of your concern." Marcell said confidently.

"Oh, that is wonderful news indeed! I only regret that Lord Overton will never meet his grandchild. Do you think you could arrange for me to call on Lady Sybella while I am here? To offer my congratulations, of course." Alcherist asked nonchalantly.

"I can try M'lord. Lord Ashrek doesn't permit her to have visitors. Concerned with the babe and all. But I will do my best Sir." Marcell said with a serious expression on his young face.

"Thank you Marcell, I have no doubt that you will." Alcherist patted the boy on his shoulder in dismissal. "Well, I'm sure you have other duties to attend to. I bid you a good night."

"You as well, M'lord." Marcell closed the door gently and headed to the kitchen.

Alcherist stood in the middle of the room, listening to Marcell's fading footsteps as he looked around at the sparsely furnished room. He had no intentions of staying in this evil place longer than necessary.

Deciding that the chair before the cold fireplace posed the least chance of being contaminated by the darkness permeating the manor, he sat to think. The fact that Sybella was with child was not lost on him. In fact, it was a wonderful turn of events. He could exact vengeance on her in the best way possible. Once he got her in his grasp, he would return to Vimeo as quickly as possible. The only thing left to plan was how.

A knock sounded at her door but the soldier didn't wait to give her time to make herself decent, he simply opened the door while a servant brushed past him with a tray.

"Your dinner Mistress. And I thought you should know that Lord Alcherist is here visiting his nephew, bringing bad news, I'm afraid." The servant placed the tray on the empty table and turned to her with a slight inclination of his head.

"Is that so. What news would that be?" Sybella sat at the table wearily; she was tired of her entrapment.

"Lord Overton is dead."

Sybella froze.

The servant boy didn't notice as he prattled on with the information he had learned. "Poisoned by King David. Lord Alcherist sends his condolences to you, also congratulations for the babe you carry. He was most pleased to hear it. He said Lord Ashrek would have to return to Vimeo to take his father's place, and I could be in charge in his absence! If that happens, I promise to release you from this confinement Mistress. Wouldn't that please you?" The servant swaggered from the room, not even taking the time to gauge Sybella's reaction to the news.

"Yes, it would please me." Sybella whispered to the closing door, "if I live that long." Placing her hand on the small roundness where her child lay, she knew Alcherist was here for one thing and one thing alone, vengeance for what she had done to his child. She was surprised the boy had survived this long. The cursed stone she had embedded beneath his hairline should have killed him in a matter of weeks. Having survived a whole year, she could only imagine the bloodthirsty state he must be in. She smiled at the thought.

<h1 style="text-align:center">Chapter 27</h1>

"ALRIC!" ELAINEA LEANED FORWARD to support his gasping frame. "Breathe Alric! Open your eyes! Please Alric, open your eyes for me! Shama, Kaison, come quickly!"

Alric's eyes fluttered before slowly opening, then darted frantically around the room before stopping on Shama.

"What happened to me?" His voice was hoarse and raw, like he'd been working in a forge, inhaling soot for years.

"You passed out after an Agiza. A dark energy ring that is released from the user of that gem in the sword. It is pure darkness, and you, unknowingly, allowed it access to you." Shama leaned over Alric, noting the fever had broken. "How do you feel now?"

Alric took stock of his body, which seemed whole, but his heart and mind felt scorched and scattered. "I feel... I don't... I'm not sure. I just need... time, please."

Shama nodded in understanding and gestured for everyone to exit the room, giving Alric the time and space to process what he had been through.

"Will he be alright?" Elainea asked Shama. She was the last to reluctantly leave his side.

"As I said, each case is different. The fact that he has awakened is good, but we have no idea of the state of his mind. He could be fractured or whole, only he can tell us. But we must not be idle while we wait, we must continue to train and find others to support our cause."

Akronius approached Shama and Elainea. Kaison sat on the ground near Naia, stroking her fur. "What exactly does this prophecy say, Shama? I think it's past time we all knew."

Shama looked around at the small band of men and animals. "You're right. No one knows exactly who first heard the prophecy, only that it was told by one coming down from the mountain and as stories tend to do, it traveled far and wide. It is said, ***When the dead King returns, darkness will follow. Evil will fill places left hollow. One throne, one life, one death to claim, one to alter, one*** *to change."* Shama's mouth flapped for a moment as if he had lost his train of thought and couldn't remember what he was saying, and then snapped shut. His brows drew together in puzzlement.

"And that means?" Elainea asked, missing the look on his face as she turned to Kaison.

"Clearly I am the dead King returned, and David must be the darkness that follows. The rest is open to much interpretation," Kaison said.

'We always assumed we had to restore the dead king to the throne. He would be the one to restore life where death once was.' Nguvu said, while Akronius translated.

"We believed Alric was the king who would be placed on the throne. Could we be wrong? Are we meant to restore you to the throne?" asked Akronius puzzled.

Shama simply looked at each member of their group, offering no clarification in either direction.

"You all must listen to your hearts, keep them turned toward The One. You have been in His presence and can recognize His guidance. Well," he stood up, "I have done what was required of me. The rest is up to you."

With those words a great gust of wind came up, dust and leaves blowing so fiercely they had to shield their eyes. When it at last died down, Shama was nowhere to be seen, he had simply vanished!

"He always knew how to make an exit," Kaison chuckled. "I suggest we table the prophecy for now and focus on doing the next right thing."

Recovering from her shock at Shama's abrupt disappearance, Elainea asked, "And that would be?"

"Spreading the word that the true King will be fighting against David and hoping there are some brave enough to answer that call," Akronius said.

Chapter 28

CHUMBRA WATCHED THE BOY sleeping in the same corner he had shoved him into several days ago. He had no use for an apprentice, but what could he do if the King didn't want to kill him?

Kicking him sharply he snapped, "Wake up, brat!"

Jacob startled awake. Chumbra smirked as he watched the memories from whatever happy dream he'd been having dissolve in the face of his current reality.

"I'm up. What should I do today?"

Chumbra glanced around. His room had never been so clean. The boy had scrubbed the floor as well as organized his bowls and vials neatly on the shelves. "Go to the kitchen. I'm sure the cook can find some use for you." He watched the skin-and-bones boy walk through the door, all elbows and knees now, but he would grow. The King should have killed him along with the rest of the family. Shaking his head, he turned toward the window. Guards were constantly patrolling the grounds. David's paranoia having reached a climax in the past few days after learning he was being blamed for the death of Lord Overton. Granted, he was not dismayed at the death, but he had no doubt it had added kindling on the blazing fire of those who were already against him. He expected an attack at every moment from anyone who so much as breathed in his direction.

Chumbra once again gathered the vial and made his way to the King's chambers. Knocking once he was bid come in.

"Is it ready?" David asked from the darkness of his room.

"Yes, my King. Prepare to be the most powerful being alive!"

"Set it on the table Chumbra. GUARD!" The king called for the man posted at his door to enter. "If anything should happen to me after taking this, you are to cut Chumbra's head off immediately. Am I clear?"

"Y..Y..Yes my King!" The guard's eyes widened in his gaunt face, his slanted lids blinking rapidly. Stepping back, he closed and locked the door without meeting Chumbra's eyes.

King David emerged from the shadows like a wraith, slinking

closer to the table. He lifted the vial and paused, pitch black eyes rose to gaze at Chumbra over the brim. "Were you able to find out what abilities Ashrek possessed to kill my mother so horrifically?"

"Err yes, your majesty. I didn't think it was still a concern of yours seeing as how you'll be so much more powerful than…" Chumbra paused his rambling as the King fixed a glare on him.

"Earth! He has an affinity for minerals and the like, he can manipulate the earth and draw minerals from rock, bone or blood to weaken or… uh kill."

"I see." He lifted the vial to his lips and tipped it back. The gelatinous goo slid into his mouth and Chumbra watched his throat convulse as he swallowed. A moment ticked by and then another, nothing appeared to be happening. Perhaps he had gotten it wrong! Chumbra wracked his brain, knowing he had gone over all the ingredients again and again.

"Mmm… mmm," the King cleared his throat and began coughing. Then he clawed at his throat as he tried in vain to breathe. He stumbled back and knocked over a chair, the trembling in his hand caused a pitcher to fall and shatter as he reached for the water. Chumbra could feel the guard step closer to his back and heard the scrape of metal as the sword left its scabbard. In the dark corner of the room David's thrashing and gasping could still be heard until…. it wasn't. Both men stood without breathing. Chumbra's eyes widened as he felt the cold blade press on the back of his neck.

"Hold," a smooth voice said, "I am well. You may leave."

Chumbra released the breath he had been holding and placed a hand on his chest as if to stop his heart from breaking through its walls.

"My King?" Chumbra asked hesitantly, the light from the open door as the soldier quickly left, momentarily caught the sinister smile of David in its thin beam before the room was once more plunged into shadow.

"No, Chumbra. I am so much more now," the voice said. Suddenly, the flames in the hearth burst to life, casting dancing shadows and heat across the room. David stepped out with a smile and held his hand out to Chumbra. "Come. Kneel and swear your loyalty."

With a look of pure glee on his face Chumbra rushed to obey. From his other pocket he withdrew a black ring, it had serpents crossing back and forth on it, and once he placed it on David's finger, they appeared to actually slither to and fro. He had found it in the treasury years ago and felt compelled to horde it, now he knew why.

"I swear my loyalty to you and you alone. Those that you hate, I will hate. Those you wish to destroy, I will destroy. My body, my will, my soul is yours to command my lord." Chumbra recited. As he kissed the ring, he felt a small prick on his lip. He rose and licked the drop of blood away. Looking into David's dark eyes he came face to face with the truth. David was no more. The black eyes that stared back into him were bottomless and held the purest form of evil possible and belonged to only one.

"Go, find me more loyal servants. We will take our rightful place as rulers of this pitiful land. No one will stand in the way of my armies. If any refuse, kill them. Tell them, their Dark Lord has returned."

Chapter 29

ALCHERIST STOOD OUTSIDE THE DOOR and could barely contain his excitement. Finally, FINALLY, he could draw his revenge from the blood of the woman who cursed his son. He opened the door slowly and stepped inside, looking around at the bare room. His eyes landed on the raven-haired woman sitting before a gentle fire, her hands resting lightly on her abdomen. Her black eyes rose and met his gaze.

"Lord Alcherist, so glad you could make the journey to our humble home despite the sad news you bring. Marcell gave me your congratulations and sympathies." She smiled demurely, "How is your family? I hear your wife and son are quite ill." The smile on her face lessened as he failed to respond as she had hoped.

"I appreciate your concern dear niece. They will be well soon, I assure you."

Alcherist walked further into the room and took the seat across from her. Crossing one leg over the other he smiled, "Sybella, Sybella, Sybella. Your father is dead, your city is under our control, your power," he gestured to her anklet, "has been stifled. You are a mere shadow of the priestess you once were." Alcherist watched as barb after barb struck her, the twinkle in her eyes disappearing entirely. "When your time is near, the child you carry will be ripped from your womb and you will die in your own blood. We will raise it far from the darkness you love so much. But I would be as barbaric as you, if I did not at least offer you the opportunity to recant your dark beliefs and give me the cure for my son. So, will you?"

Sybella looked at the man across from her. He had changed in the months since his son was returned. He was hard now, calloused by the life he had been thrust into, but he was still no match for her or the one she believed in.

"Alcherist, thank you so much for your offer, but you should know better than to think I would EVER betray my lord." She smiled at the small tick that started just beneath his left eye. "He is returning soon and I will be found faithful. You will be nothing more than dust beneath our feet."

"I wish I could say your answer surprises me, but since it doesn't, perhaps this will surprise you." Leaning forward he whispered, "I am going to convince my nephew that there is no safer place for you in your delicate state, than at my home where you will be cut off from all connections to the Dark Lord and his followers. You will be cared for as one of my own, in a room set up specifically for you. Won't that be wonderful?"

Alcherist smiled as he watched Sybella's eyes grow just a little larger, as he finished talking. "We will be leaving in a few days, so pack what little you have. I am so looking forward to spending time with you, we have so much to discuss."

Sybella clasped her hands tightly together as Alcherist left the room. She hated feeling helpless. There had to be a way she could regain some of her power. If only she had access to her books.

Alcherist made his way to his nephew's room and knocked. There was no answer, so he knocked again, harder. When there was still no answer, he opened the door and stepped inside. Sprawled across a table with an overturned cup just out of reach of his hand, lay Ashrek.

"Weak fool." Alcherist shook his head in disgust. He walked over to the night stand and lifted a pitcher of water. Approaching the inebriated man, he overturned the contents of the pitcher and smiled as Ashrek sputtered into consciousness.

"What, ugh, what are you doing here?" He slurred, wiping his face with a dirty sleeve.

"Forgive me nephew, as much as I hate to intrude on your… grieving, we need to discuss our next steps. This affront cannot go unanswered! You must avenge your father." Alcherist watched his nephew stumble about the room looking for clean clothes.

"Nephew, it is no secret your father was not as supportive of you as he should have been. I understand your grief and frustration at the loss of any possibility to make amends to that fact." Ashrek grunted in response as he struggled to get a clean shirt over his large frame. "I tried to get him to come see you, to acknowledge the amazing job you have done here in securing your rule. He was a stubborn man and would not listen, but I'm here. I see what you have done with these evil people and I'm *proud* of you. Let me help you finish what you have started here."

Ashrek looked at his uncle with gratitude, slumping heavily into a chair. "Thank you Uncle, your words are most welcome in this troubling time. What did you have in mind?"

"Allow me to take Sybella back with me. If David mounts an attack on you, he can't be allowed to claim her. In the wrong hands and with access to her dark arts once more, she would be too strong. I will keep her under constant guard until your child is born and then... we'll see where we stand. You should focus on the steadfastness of your new army. I'll bring word back to Vimeo that you want your soldiers to join you here for preparations. After all, you are now the new lord of Vimeo, they are yours to command."

Ashrek turned and gazed into the fire for a few moments, "You're right Uncle. My father underestimated me, but he is no longer here to make the same mistake again. I'll have her prepared to travel with you at first light. I'm sure David is preparing to attack us as we speak, I must prepare my army." Looking at his uncle for a moment, "Uncle, I am aware of your feelings toward her. Once the child is born, she is yours to do with as you wish. Killing Vicrano was necessary. I hope this will make up for that."

"Thank you, Nephew. I will not say I'll enjoy her death for violence has never suited me. You know this, but I will extract the cure for your cousin and then make her death a quick one. Thank you for understanding where your father could not."

Alcherist dipped his head in deference and left the room smiling.

Chapter 30

ALRIC SAT IN THE SHADOWS of the tree line, wrapped in a thick cloak and watched his sister and Akronius run through a series of drills. She was a natural with her flaming sword and Akronius was the perfect one to train her. Glancing to the other side, he saw his father with the wolf pack. They sat conversing in silence, and by the river a pile of stones that was really Syphra, sat with Auni. Everyone had their place. They were so sure of who they were and what they were meant to be doing. Everyone, but him. Thinking back on his time in the crucible, he had been forced to admit his doubt of The One and of himself, but even that had not offered any clarity and he desperately wanted it, needed it.

A twig snapping in the forest behind him broke the silence.
Alric glanced to each side and saw figures moving through the shadows. Shifting as slowly as he could, he moved to brace himself against a tree. Closing his eyes, he tried to settle his inner voice to channel a vision as Shama had taught him. When he opened his eyes, it was as if he were in a dream, he could see himself leaning on the tree and the shadows moving around him, one in particular was getting closer to his position. Taking a deep breath, he ended the vision. Finding himself in his body once more, he estimated the time until the person would pass near him.

Springing out from the shadow of the tree, he surrounded his captive in a shield and lifted him off the forest floor.

"Oh, ummm, who are you?" He could not mask his surprise at finding his captive to be a woman! A very small, very angry woman at that.

"Let me go or they'll kill you where you stand," she said evenly, not at all deterred by her captive state.

"They?" Alric said. Looking around he saw several men emerge from the shadows with swords drawn and directed toward him. "Is that so?" he said with a smile. He whistled once and within moments the wolves had the men surrounded.

"Tell them to sheath their blades, or *they* will kill them where they stand," Alric said proudly.

The woman audibly growled and reluctantly told her men to drop their swords. Then they were herded into the small yard, Alric still floating the woman in a tightly held shield.

Akronius approached them at a quick jog. "Which way does the river flow?"

"From the south." The woman answered with a smirk in Alric's direction.

"Release her Alric. Nguvu, Naia. They are allies."

Alric slowly did as he was instructed. "Who is she, and why were they skulking around in the forest?"

"I told you we had to gather those loyal to our cause. I left word at the village for any interested to meet us here, with a coded message. I wasn't sure if any would show up so I didn't tell you."

Turning to the woman he said, "My apologies, miss. What is your name?"

Giving Alric a scathing look, she brushed the dust off her clothes as if to rid herself of the unpleasant encounter. "I'm Keuri and these are my men. We're few, but strong and loyal." Giving Alric her back she addressed Kaison and Elainea. "We're from the south and have been sent to aid you. We don't want this evil to breach our borders as well."

"We appreciate the assistance. I am Akronius and my familiar is down by the river. This is Kaison and his familiar, Naia. Elainea is there with the flaming sword and you've already met Alric."

Keuri nodded in greeting with each introduction. "As I said, I am Keuri." With a wave of her hand, the wind lifted her short white hair and blew in the direction of a dark-skinned bald man. "This is Zee, he doesn't speak, but despite that he is sure to get his point across." The man smiled exposing long serpentine teeth, touching his scaled forehead in a small salute with trim nails that elongated into sharp claws. "That is Bjorn, he can affect the weight of almost anything except his own." Keuri said with a smirk at the thick-waisted man. To prove her point, Bjorn focused his red eyed gaze on the sword Elainea was holding and though she tried, she quickly found herself straining as it fell from her hand with a thud. She gestured to another brown skinned woman with purple coiled hair. "This is Sarta, Alric you may want to step back for this...or not," she said with a wider grin. Sarta returned the smile as she lifted her hand to the sky, swirling her fingers and motioned like she was pulling something to her. Immediately lightning struck in a circle around where she stood, deadly and graceful. "Lastly is Eret." She gestured to a short stocky man with red hair and matching freckles across his sand colored face. Kneeling down he placed his hand palm down on the ground, everyone looked for something to hold on to as it began to shake beneath them.

Turning to face Kaison, they all took a knee, "We're at your service, my King."

Kaison looked uncomfortable at the acknowledgment. "Well, ah, your help is most welcome Keuri, but you see... I'm not King anymore. My son, Alric is destined for the throne." All eyes turned to Alric.

"What?" Keuri shouted, "You cannot be serious. He's a boy!"

"Thank you Keuri for that lesson in the obvious." Alric said, "I can assure you, I hold the same reservations, but it would seem my father and The One think otherwise."

"Yes well... Keuri, you can follow me." Elainea said softly, "You all must be tired from your journey. I have some food and water inside." Elainea tried to defuse the situation and took the guests inside.

"Well, that went well," Alric sighed.

"We will have to convince them," Akronius said.

Chapter 31

THE DARK LORD NOW HAD full control of the body which had once belonging to David, and stood before a crowd of his loyal followers. Garbed in a robe that matched his dark eyes and inscribed with symbols from a long forgotten language in red embroidery on the edges. Not a hair was out of place as he looked on the people gathered before him. Each lip bore a dark spot where they had kissed his ring and taken his oath. His dark eyes roamed over each person, looking for a weakness and finding none.

"You have sworn your allegiance to me this day, pledging your lives, your bodies and your very souls to my cause. Go back to your villages, your homes. Look for those who would betray me. Expose your neighbors, your friends. Even those you call family *must* be made to understand who holds the true power in Elhaanai! I will expand my dungeons for any who refuse to be persuaded."

David raised his hand over the crowd and began to chant, in response his shadow began to grow and stretch. It split and slithered between the rows of men and women, merging and disappearing into their own shadows. "Where you go, I will go, when you speak, it will be me speaking. You are mine."

"WE ARE YOURS!" The room reverberated with the sound of stomping feet and shouts. King David smiled as he walked down a side passage to his chambers.

"Chumbra, come here." David said to the empty room. It was only a few moments before the sound of running feet met his ears.

"Yes, My Lord. How can I serve you?" Chumbra had heard the whisper as if they had been standing together, not in opposite ends of the manor, and had come immediately.

"I have a priestess in Arcana, Sybella. She has always been a very loyal daughter to me. I need her. You will get her for me."

"Sybella? She is being held captive by Lord Ashrek, my lord. How am I to… aaaarrrrrgghhh," Chumbra gurgled as he clawed at his throat. It felt like a hand was squeezing and he felt his toes scrape against the floor as he struggled against the invisible vice lifting him into the air.

"Do **not** question me Chumbra. You are not only insignificant to me, but also replaceable." Though Chumbra stood just inside the doorway and David stood in the center of the room, he could feel his breath brushing against his cheek with each threatening word. "Bring me Sybella!"

The hold on his neck released and he dropped to his knees, gasping for air.

"Yes, my, Lord." Chumbra responded as he scurried from the room.

Turning to the mirror, King David looked admiringly at his reflection. This host was much more fitting than the last, time would tell if it would stand up to the rigors necessary to gain control of Elhaanai.

"Enjoying the show?" He laughed as the David in the reflection pounded on the glass, screaming inaudibly. "You should get comfortable. This will not be over quickly. If you behave, I may even let you out for a bit every now and again."

Turning from the mirror and the sobbing man kneeling in its reflection, he sat in a large chair facing the fireplace. Leaning forward he blew onto the dying embers, causing them to glow and come back to life. Settling once more with a sigh, he closed his eyes to enjoy the heat.

Chumbra raced back to his room, leaning heavily on the door as he closed it. Logically, he knew there was no place he could hide from the Dark Lord, but fear overruled him. How was he to get to Sybella? He knew she was held under lock and key by Ashrek. His spies had told him she even had an anklet that prevented her from using her gift. He was sure she no longer had access to her texts or scrolls but he had to reach her somehow. Pacing the length of his room again and again, pulling on his hair, he berated himself.

'Think! Think! Think! Alcherist murdered his own brother and blamed it on David. He probably hopes this will cause Ashrek to attack us, but why would he want Ashrek to attack us? Arcana is already deeply rooted in worship of the Dark Lord, they are of no concern to us. But Vimeo is not... he would have to return there to prepare his men to meet an attack from us. That would leave Arcana

110

unprotected... Sybella unprotected. No, no. She is with child. He would never let her far from his sight or the sight of one he trusted! YES! Either he'll leave his uncle in Arcana as her caretaker or he will allow his uncle to take her back to Vimeo. The CHILD! Of course! Alcherist's son was cursed by her, now it all becomes clear. Ashrek will leave Vimeo in his uncle's hands and he will keep Arcana. Sybella will be forced to cure Khal in the process.'

"Of Course!" Chumbra shouted, as he began preparations for his journey to Vimeo. "Thank you," he whispered in relief to no one in particular and stumbled when the sinister reply came.

'You're Welcome.'

Chapter 32

SYBELLA HAD NEVER REALLY WANTED children. Even when her father pressured her into marriage and constantly nagged her about it. She was not the 'nurturing' type and yet, she found herself speaking to the child within her, caressing her ever growing belly and smiling with those first flutters of movement. The spell she cast would speed up the pregnancy, but she didn't tell Ashrek that. Hopefully he would be too ill to notice and by the time she gave birth, he would be near death.

"Don't get attached." Ashrek said as he walked in and observed her in one of those secret moments. "He's mine. You'll never lay eyes on his face. You will die before you can contaminate the first breath he draws."

She hid how much she hated him with a smile. "As you say, My Lord." As she listened to him cough, she knew he'd gone to a healer about it. But it would do him no good. He would be dead before her child took his first breath, not she.

Ashrek cleared his throat once more and wiped the sweat from his brow. Being in this cursed land was bad for his health as well as his soul. But all the temples had been destroyed, every book honoring the Dark Lord and The One had been burned along with any followers who refused to recant. He hoped the purification would bring healing to the land and to his body.

"My uncle will be returning home tomorrow. You will go with him. You'll remove whatever curse you've placed on my cousin and stay under their care until it is time for you to give birth."

Sybella bowed her head in acknowledgment, as she had been expecting this. It wouldn't make a difference, no matter what her location or proximity to Ashrek, the power would still find its way to her. She could feel it building up, begging for release. When the time came, it would be glorious!

"Pack your things, what little remains," he said looking around the room. "He'll come for you when he's ready to depart."

Ashrek left Sybella to her minuscule packing, pausing outside her door to catch his breath. Leaning against the wall for support, he could not shake this weak feeling. The healers could do nothing for him, saying he needed rest after experiencing so much loss and trauma. No, he was not an emotional or weak man, she had done this. He knew it. Somehow, she had found a way to curse him, but she would not win. He would not let her. Whatever it took, he would find a cure for this mysterious ailment.

Slowly making his way to the other end of the manor, Ashrek again had to pause before entering his uncle's room. He could not allow his weakened state to show, he knew even family would attack at the first sign of vulnerability.

"Uncle, Sybella has been told of the change in location and will be ready when you're set to leave. Do you need anything else from me? Will you be able to pass the message along to the troops to meet me at the mountain pass when the time comes?" Ashrek knew his uncle was not war minded. He had his doubts about his ability to stir the hearts of men for battle.

"Ashrek, if I didn't know better, I would say you doubted me. You worry too much. I'll do exactly what needs to be done when it needs to be done. The men will be ready and eager to dethrone the menace of Elhaanai. You have nothing to worry about." Alcherist looked more closely at his nephew who was sweating and seemed to be having difficulty breathing. "Are you alright Nephew? You seem unwell?"

"No, no Uncle. I'm fine, just a little tired. I haven't been resting well since the news of my father's death. It has left me feeling... unsettled."

"Yes, I understand that. Remember, he is at peace now and we will avenge him. The one responsible will be within our grasp soon enough. You should go to bed. I'll see you before departing in the morning."

"You're right, and I do trust you Uncle. Like me, father underestimated you as well. Good night."

"Yes, yes he did. Good night Ashrek." Alcherist said softly. As the door closed, he turned to gaze out the window.

You both underestimate me, nephew. I'm far stronger and more cunning than you ever thought I could be. More than I even thought I could become. I will finally live the life I was meant to with my family. My son and my wife, they will be made well and it will all have been worth it. I just have to see this through, and then it will be over. It will all be over.'

Chapter 33

"HOW LONG HAVE YOU LIVED HERE?" Keuri asked Elainea. "We grew up here. Our mother is buried here. It is our home." Elainea said as she placed a second loaf of bread on the table and watched Zee as he cut a slice with one sharp claw.

"I have never heard of or seen gifts like yours. Is everyone in the south like you?" Elainea asked.

"Not really, but we southerners tend to be gifted with affinities of the elements or nature. Zee here, inherited his gifts from his parents. His mother was a familiar to a snake and his father, to a bear; so, the scales and retractable claws. He has no familiar and clearly does not need one. The others, myself included, come from families that were not gifted at all and still, we somehow manifested. What about you?"

"My mother was a scribe, a record keeper of sorts. I have control over fire, botany and can cast a few spells. Alric's mother was a strong priestess of The One and a seer. He inherited that gift along with casting barriers, as you witnessed." Elainea was not completely convinced that she could trust them, and decided not to explain how they could share their gifts.

Zee performed a series of hand movements and Eret interpreted. "He asks, how do you not have the same mother? You're siblings."

"That is true, but Alric's mother performed a spell and placed him in *my* mother's, Wleia's, womb to save his life. It's a long story for another time. We're siblings in the only way that matters to us. I will defend him with my life and he mine. He is meant to be king. I'll see that he is." Elainea said as she locked eyes with Keuri, who nodded and smiled slightly. It was not convincing. The others all returned to finishing the meal set before them, eyes down and lost in their own thoughts of the future.

"How do we know we can trust them?" Kaison asked Akronius as he sat by the barn, drawing a whetstone against the edge of his blade. "It's no secret that after the great war southerners stayed to themselves. Why come to our aid now?"

"We need all the help we can get, Kaison. Maybe what they say is true. We know David will not be satisfied conquering Elhaanai alone. He's already gearing up to attack Vimeo and perhaps Arcana as well. The south will be his next target if he succeeds here. So I guess they're looking out for themselves in a way."

"That is true, but they didn't seem convinced about Alric being on the throne and sadly, my son seems to agree with them." Kaison's shoulders dropped. "I can't help but feel responsible for his lack of confidence. If I or his mother had been present to raise him…"

"There's nothing you can do about the past. We can only do our best for where we are right now." Akronius stood, stretching as he looked toward the sunset. "Hopefully, more people will join us in the coming days. I think we are running out of time."

Akronius walked down to the river and to anyone observing, it would look as though he were resting against a pile of rocks not a full-grown dragon.

'Syphra, what do you think of these newcomers?'

'Intentions are always hard to discern without first seeing actions. They're here and say they'll help. We can only watch, wait and hope. Would you like to practice with me tonight? You have done well so far.'

'Yes, I am much more comfortable on your back now, but we'll have to find a saddle of some sort before battle. We can try a partial shift again.'

Akronius started his deep breathing as Syphra had instructed him to do. Focusing on the connection between them, he could feel her heat flowing through his veins. Then the pain began, bones cracked and muscles stretched and twisted. It did not cause him to pass out like it had the first time, but sweat still dripped down his face as he grunted from the effort.

'Well done Akronius.'

Looking down he saw his hands replaced with two blue scaled claws, smaller versions of Syphra's and just as sharp. Proud of himself he opened and closed them. Placing them on the ground, he raked the earth and left deep gouges. This skill would be useful in hand-to-hand combat.

'Hold the form for as long as you're able. Think about how it feels in this form, how your mind is focused. Feel the muscles as you move. They're part of you, an extension of your arm.'

Akronius moved his hands around more and held it as long as he was able before releasing the connection on an exhale.

'Well done. You were able to hold it far longer than the last time. Just think how it will feel when you completely transform and we fly together. It is an experience I look forward to sharing with you.'

'I look forward to it as well. Good night, Syphra.'

Stretching his arms over his head, Akronius groaned and headed to the barn. It had been converted to accommodate him and their new guests. Settling down with his back to the wall nearest the door, no one would be able to pass him without his knowing.

Chapter 34

SYBELLA SAT COMFORTABLY ATOP HER dappling mare, surrounded by guards, following Lord Alcherist. They had left before the sun had crested the horizon, with no opportunity given to break her fast. Alcherist's mistreatment of her had begun. Plodding along, she observed her captor. She could sense he was different, strong but darker as well. Dawn came and went without them stopping. Noon saw the full force of the sun beating down on their heads. Although winter still held them in its grasp, she found herself sweating and increasingly irritated. Glancing around her, she saw that the soldiers had food packed and were nibbling away as well as drinking from water skins. So that was to be the way of it then. Alcherist had no intention of stopping, he would let her go hungry and thirsty.

"Alcherist, My Lord. Could we stop for a moment?" Sybella humbly requested, well as much as she could bring herself to.

"No." He responded without even glancing her way.

"I need to stop." She tried once more.

"No." Again he said, with an irritated glance her way.

"Lord Alcherist. I highly doubt your nephew would want anything to happen to his unborn child. I *need* to *stop now!*" Sybella said firmly with her head held high, pulling on the reins to bring her mount to a stop, forcing the guards to stop as well or collide with her.

Wheeling his black steed around he approached and circled her, causing her own mare to shy anxiously. "Woman, your *needs* are not a concern of mine. If you need to relieve yourself, go ahead, just like the animal that you are. We won't be stopping until we are within the walls of my manor. And then I will offer you *every* comfort that you *deserve.*" He sneered and spat in her direction before resuming his position in front of the small group. The guard nearest her leaned forward and gave a tug on the reigns she held to start her horse's forward movement once more.

Sybella set her face firmly and determined to deny him the satisfaction of fulfilling his crude suggestion. She would find a way to make him pay, right along with his nephew. She whispered a prayer to the Dark Lord for an opportunity and the ability to do it.

'I hear you daughter. Be patient. Our time will come.'

Sybella was shocked, speechless. In all her years as a faithful servant of the Dark Lord he had never, *ever* spoken so clearly to her. She was so happy she couldn't contain the cackle that burst from her mouth. Lord Alcherist turned to look at her and she blew a kiss his way. She would wait, oh yes, she would wait.

Chumbra had left immediately after figuring out where Sybella would be taken. He had acquired a room near the gate to watch for her impending arrival. He wandered for several days acclimating himself to the town surrounding Damu Manor and the general feel of the people. Most mourned the death of Lord Overton, but there was a growing pocket of those who doubted Alcherist's version of his death. It was into that group that he inserted himself and fanned the flames of dissent.

"Why should we believe what Alcherist says? He has never been our leader. He was always the weaker of the brothers. You know that, something is wrong here! I'm sure of it," one man said to another over a tankard of ale. Chumbra sat in a dark corner listening intently, his face hidden within the shadow of his cloak.

"Exactly! He *is* weak! There is no way he could come up with and carry out a plot as elaborate as you are suggesting. The man is a puppet, always has been. I would not be surprised if he was in cahoots with that madman David. We need Lord Ashrek to come back, he will follow in his father's footsteps," the other man said, slamming his mug down.

"Gentlemen, may I buy your next round?" Chumbra sidled up to their table and signaled the barmaid to bring more ale. "I couldn't help overhearing your conversation and thought I could offer some... clarification."

The men eyed him suspiciously as the drinks were brought to the table. "And just who are you?"

"I am Cyrus, I lived in Elhaanai but left to escape the rule of that madman. His guards razed my village to the ground. I barely escaped with my life!"

119

"Madness!"

"Terrible!"

"Unbelievable!"

The men at the table murmured around him but drew closer to hear the details, as he knew they would.

"Yes, it was a terrible ordeal. But on my journey here, I did hear from several sources that Alcherist *did* kill his own brother in exchange for Sybella. You know she cursed his wife and son. The poor man is blinded by his desire for revenge. It's a shame, really." Chumbra pretended to take a deep pull from his mug as the chattering began all around him. "Imagine that dark worshiper here in Vimeo! She is a danger to everyone!"

"True!"

"Evil woman."

"She's a murderer!"

"...not gonna stand for this!"

"No better than a traitor!"

Around and around the words went, swirling venom from one mouth to the others' ears. Alcherist would be hard pressed to get within the city walls with Sybella in tow, and then he would make his move.

Chapter 35

"WALK WITH ME." Kaison said quietly to Alric as he headed toward the river. Both were silent, listening to the crackling of ice on the slowly freezing river and the trill of birds in the trees. "Do you want to be king, Alric?"

The question caused Alric to fall slightly behind his father out of surprise. No one had ever asked him what *he* wanted. He had only been told who he was and what he was meant to do and be.

"It's not that I do not *want* to be king, Father. I'm just not sure I *can* be king."

"That is not what I asked you." Kaison stopped and looked across the river at the woods. "Alric, without using your gift, what do you see over there?"

"Trees, rocks, darkness."

"Good, now use your sight and tell me what you see."

"The same thing."

"No, look deeper. Pay attention."

"Big trees, big rocks." Alric glanced over at his father and cringed. "Okay, I see some birds in the trees. There are a few empty nests, smaller animals and deer walking through the forest, light coating of snow on the ground..."

"Better, what you see is *life,* Alric. For years we've been *told* that the woods are cursed, abandoned with no explanation. We've been *told* all who enter will never return. But those creatures you see live there, because they have been immersed in it and know it, rather than fear it. It's where your mother was heading when she was killed. The unknown can be feared only until it becomes known, Alric." Kaison turned to his son. "I'm sorry I wasn't able to immerse you in the knowledge of what it means to be a good king. But you have to decide, now, if this is the path for you. If you want *life,* or if you want fear."

With a final squeeze of his shoulder, Kaison left him to his thoughts.

Gazing across the frozen water, Alric thought back to the crucible and the questions he had been asked. He trusted The One, what he needed was to trust himself as well. Glancing back at his home, so many depending on him, and beyond this small plot of land, even more that he did not know. He turned once more toward the far shore. His mother had known something about what lay within the far wood. It must be important. Making his decision he drew his coat closer around his shoulders and took the first step.

Elainea had watched Kaison walk away with her brother and return alone. Glancing further down river she could just make out his shape, the early morning snow casting him in shadow. Her heart stuttered in her chest as she watched him take a step toward the river, and then another.

"No. No, no, no! ALRIC!" Elainea shouted and ran toward the river even though she knew she wouldn't make it to him in time. She had no idea what Kaison could have said to him to make him walk into the freezing water. Slowing, she met Alric's eyes as he turned to her, waist deep in the water and smiled from the short distance now between them. She watched as the water flowed around him and the shield he had erected. He continued walking until the water completely covered him. Several tense moments passed before she saw him emerge on the other side of the river. He raised a hand and walked into the cursed woods.

SLAM! The door flew open and crashed against the wall. "WHAT did you say to my brother that would cause him to cross the river and go *into* the cursed woods?" Elainea was furious, her hair floated around as waves of heat poured off her skin causing everyone to back up several steps for fear of being scorched.

All eyes turned to Kaison. "He did what?" Akronius whispered.

"He chose life." Kaison said with a smile, glancing around at everyone's confusion. "Alric doesn't trust himself to be king, he doesn't think he's strong enough. The crucible helped to dispel some of those doubts, but he has to face the rest if he wants to reach his full potential. He's going into the woods to do that."

"But it is cursed isn't it?" Akronius asked.

"Not really, that's a rumor that started after the dire wolves were hunted to near extinction. There is a place in the center of the forest that seers pilgrimage to in order to commune directly with The One. It is where Alanna was most likely running to when she was killed. If he can reach it, he'll find the strength and purpose he's been searching for."

Akronius glanced down at the mention of Alanna. He did not know if he would ever forgive himself for that moment in his past. He was still a work in progress. He whispered a silent prayer that Alric would succeed where his mother could not.

Chapter 36

CRESTING THE HILL, LORD ALCHERIST saw his home in the distance and exhaled the breath he had been holding since leaving Arcana. Feeling eyes on his back, he straightened once more in his saddle.

"We're almost home men! Warm beds and ale for every soldier tonight! Ride!" The men cheered in response and Sybella smirked as her mount was urged into a trot.

She kept her hands wrapped around the pommel, glancing down every so often at her ring. From it, small streaks of black made their way from her knuckle to her wrist to her forearm and up. She could feel the power pulsing through her veins, strengthening her and her unborn child. Ashrek would probably be bedridden by now, weak with fatigue and fear. She wished she could see it; his face as gaunt as hers once was, struggling for each breath. She would wait for word of his death and rejoice when it came.

The gates were wide open when Alcherist and his men reached them. Smiling, he strutted proudly through them. The silence and stares that greeted him were a far cry from the waves of cheers and accolades he had ridden out to. He could hear whispers swelling in the crowds.

"Sir, we should ride quickly. This crowd is not for you." The captain of the guard rode closely to him, tensely gripping the handle of his sword. No sooner had the words left his mouth than he was smacked in the face with rotten produce. Behind him he heard shouting and turned in time to see a bucket of human waste dumped from a window above them and land on one of the other men.

"RIDE OUT! ARROWHEAD!" The captain shouted and soldiers formed an inverted V, placing himself at point, Lord Alcherist and Sybella at the center and one guard behind. "Make Way! MOVE!" Using their horses as battering rams they forced their way through the angry mob.

"MURDERER!"

"TRAITORS!"

"Kill her!"

"Kill them all!"

Alcherist could hear the screams all around them, what had happened while he was gone? Rounding the bend in the road, he saw the manor ahead, at the same time a scream sounded from behind. The soldier bringing up the rear had been torn from his mount and was being pummeled by the enraged people. Looking to his side, Sybella met his eyes and smiled. She was leaning all the way forward as they galloped through the gate which quickly slammed shut behind them.

"WHAT IS GOING ON?" Alcherist roared as servants scurried to take their horses. Storming into the manor he looked for his steward.

"Bastien! Where are you? Someone Find Bastien Right Now!" Alcherist dragged Sybella behind him into the war room and thrust her into a chair, her hands bound in her lap. Impatiently pacing from one side of the room to the other, he ran his hands through his graying hair in frustration.

"Welcome back My Lord." Bastien said, rushing into the room wringing his hands.

"What happened?" Alcherist stood with his hands clenched at his sides and waited.

"Sir... I'm not... you see... the people…" Bastien stuttered.

"SPIT IT OUT!" Alcherist shouted.

Swallowing audibly, he continued, "The people somehow heard you would be bringing *her* back with you. Everyone knows who she is and whom she serves. They think you have joined with King David and she is a gift to him. You are being called a traitor."

Sybella chuckled in her seat. "Well, whatever will we do now, My Lord?"

"Bastien, accompany the guard and escort the prisoner to her cell please."

"Yes, My Lord." Bowing slightly, he exited the room behind the guard and Sybella. They walked down the hallway, listening to the screams coming in through the shuttered windows.

"You'll be staying here, Miss." Bastien said holding the cell door open, then, quickly closed it behind Sybella as she looked around.

"Hands." The guard said, cutting the ropes as she placed them near the bars. Rubbing her wrists, she watched the torch light fade away with the sound of their footsteps. She was not afraid of the dark.

It was like coming home to her, comforting.

Sitting on the threadbare cot that was placed against the wall, she looked up at the slit in the top of the wall, closing her eyes as a sliver of daylight cut across her face.

One hand on her stomach, she felt a small push where it rested and thought it could be the hand of her child. "Yes, little one, keep your hand in mine. We'll be fine."

Tracking the sunlight's path across her cell, the day passed in silence. She was hungry, thirsty and offended by the smell from the bucket in the corner. She was a prisoner and had not expected to be catered to, but human decency would have been enough.

She felt the hair on her arms stand up and a prickle on her scalp. Holding her breath, she glanced around and waited for the magic to manifest itself.

'Sybella.'

"Who are you?"

'A servant of the Dark Lord, like you.'

"And what do you want?"

'Nothing. An opportunity to free yourself will come. The Dark Lord requires your freedom.'

"When will this opportunity come?"

'Soon. Be ready.'

She felt the air in the room cool as the presence dissipated. Smiling again and she caressed her belly and cooed to the child growing within,

"See, I told you we would be fine." Curling onto her side she waited and rested.

Chumbra exhaled and relaxed out of his meditation pose. Essence casting was draining and he had very little time to rest. He had to move. The cogs were in place and needed only a small push.

Chapter 37

'I KNEW SHE WAS WORRIED, even though I had promised to protect her. She was the stronger one and a natural caretaker. I couldn't continue to live like this, the weight was pressing on me and with each new day I felt like giving in a little more.

I smiled and laughed, but inside I was broken, like a glass shattered into a million pieces. If they could see into my soul, they would see the bits and pieces being held together by tattered threads. Who am I? Am I just who they say I am or something, SOMEONE more? Will I be strong enough? What happens if I fail? What happens if I succeed?'

Glancing one last time at Elainea standing on the far bank, Alric stepped into the tree line and disappeared. It was as if he stepped into a different world. The trees were taller and wider than any he had ever seen. And it was quiet, so quiet. He was the intruder and all of nature watched him, warily.

He placed a hand on a nearby tree and quickly removed it. It felt like the tree was trying to suck him in. Using his sight, he looked down and through the earth. The roots were all twisted and wound around each other. There was no distinction between the roots of one tree and its neighbor. The entire forest was connected like veins, and he knew he had to find the heart. Tentatively, he replaced his hand and closed his eyes, *'please show me the way.'*

He felt his gift activate and steal his breath with its intensity. It was unlike anything he'd ever felt. Opening his white eyes, the path lay before him, misty and winding.

When he removed his hand, his eyes cleared and the path vanished, but he felt a directional pull that strengthened with his first step. The pull increased with each step. Deeper into the woods he went. So focused on the pull, he didn't notice the shadows closing in on him from each side.

SNAP!

Whipping his head to the side, he stumbled as he locked eyes with something tracking him.

"Grrrrrr!"

His eyes widened as he looked to the other side and saw another set of glowing eyes in the dim light. Stopping, he looked around and knew he was surrounded. One by one the wolves stepped from the shadows. These were not the dire wolves he had grown accustomed to; these were closer to hell hounds. Except for Syphra, their teeth were sharper and longer than any he had seen. Their fur was matted and missing in spots, ribs visible beneath taut skin.

Circling him, the saliva dropped from their curling lips. Alric didn't know how he knew, but as the first one lunged at him, he instinctively erected a shield and the creature bounced off with a yelp. One by one, each animal tested the strength of his shield, scratching and trying to bite it. At each point of attack, Alric focused on securing it only to find with increasing frequency that another would attack simultaneously from a different place. Sweat began to drip down his face and he had to draw the shield in closer to his body, allowing the wolves to draw closer. The one that seemed to be in charge paused in his attack, then snarled at the others. They attacked harder and faster. Alric once again drew the shield closer to himself. This went on for hours until he was looking down the throats of his attackers and his arms and legs trembled from exertion. The shield was as close to his body as it could be. Soon, they would be through and at his throat.

"If you're here, if you called me to this path, please save me. Please," Alric whispered, eyes squeezed in concentration. On the other side of the barrier, the wolves paused in their attack. Backing up a few feet, they looked up as Alric felt a breeze ruffle his hair, a large shadow hovered above them. Alric felt the shield failing, slipping through his hold like water. Sensing his vulnerability, the alpha leaped at him, jaws wide and claws extended, only to be plucked midair by large talons and thrown to the forest floor. Falling back, Alric gazed up into the translucent eyes of a Haliaeetus. It landed over him as a mother would her chicks. Spreading its wings and lowering its head. The wolves were no match for the powerful beak facing them. With a final snarl, they skulked back into the shadows. Alric gazed up at this bird that until this moment had lived only in the legends of his people. It had pure white wings edged in gold, its eyes were pools of amber and glinted with understanding. The sharp talons on its feet could crush a man with little effort but instead rested on either side of him, protecting him.

Once clear of danger, the large bird tucked its wings to its side and looked down at an exhausted Alric. They held eye contact for a heartbeat, and then it gently placed one talon around him, lifting him off the ground and into the air with one beat of its massive wings and a cry that pierced his soul.

The view was magnificent. Looking up into the clouds, Alric whispered his thanks to The One for such an unexpected savior. Seeing a clearing below, they began their descent and the bird hovered near the ground and released him from its hold. Landing and standing off to the side, its eyes shifted to something just behind Alric, bowed its head, and then with a sound like a thousand beating wings it launched majestically into the air once more.

Alric could feel the hair on the back of his neck prick and was afraid to turn around. He had reached the heart of the forest. Turning, he saw a large tree in the center of the clearing. Its roots were both above and below the earth, and pulsed with a brilliant white light. Its branches were as thick as a man's waist and covered in leaves that were broader and lusher and greener than any he had ever seen, untouched by the frost in the surrounding forest. From the trunk of the tree, a figure emerged and walked toward him. He could not tell if it was a man or a woman, old or young. The closer to him it got, the heavier his soul felt, eventually Alric could do nothing but kneel under the pressure. As the figure stood before him tears began to flow as he recognized the feeling radiating toward him.

'Alric.'

The voice was gentle but firm, it was like the warmest hug. It wrapped around him and reached deep inside where he was wounded and struggling with self-doubt.

"Yes, my Lord."

Chapter 38

EVEN THOUGH NIGHT HAD FALLEN, small clusters of men still walked the streets. Torches cast shadows across their angry faces. Stopping at one group and then another, Chumbra stirred the simmering feelings in everyone he came in contact with. Watering the seeds of doubt and mistrust against Lord Alcherist, the grumbling grew louder and the groups larger. It did not take long for a mob to form and head to the gates of the manor to demand Sybella be handed over to them. She would recant her faith in the Dark Lord or accept their judgment on her life.

"We need more men at the gate! They cannot be allowed to breach the walls! Hold men, HOLD!" the captain yelled as soldiers raced across the courtyard. From a high window, Lord Alcherist watched with disgust that was slowly turning to fear. He had no training in controlling such mobs. His brother would have put a swift end to this madness. It was only a matter of time before they broke through the gate. He would hand her over to them for them to tear her apart after she healed his son.

Rushing to her cell, he found her reclining and humming lightly. The echoes of the yells reached her even here. "Looks like you're having some trouble with your people My Lord. I'm sure your *brother* would not have had these problems, but oops, he's dead isn't he. Are you still grieving my lord? No, I don't think you are."

"Shut up!" He unlocked her cell door, grabbing her arm roughly and dragged her to the stairs. "You will heal my son and then I'm handing you over to the crowd. They can tear you limb from limb for all I care."

Reaching the nursery, he stood with her arm still clenched tightly in his fist. "Do it."

"Of course, My Lord." She walked over to the cage that held the child and unlocked it.

"NO! Don't open," his jaw dropped as he watched her reach in and lift the child into her arms. Khal gazed up at her adoringly, drool sliding between his sharp teeth and down his chin.

"Hush now, Aunt Sybella will make it all better little one." Looking up to meet Alcherist's eyes as she placed a kiss on the child's clammy head, she smiled at the barely contained rage she saw there. With one hand, she brushed the spot where she had placed the cursed stone and it vanished. Instantly, the child's eyes changed back to green and the adoration turned to terrified crying.

"Ugh, he is restored. Take him. With his healing, your wife will return to her normal self in time as well." She handed the squalling child to its father, a small place in her black heart warmed at the sight. Turning her back to the scene, she stifled it, "Now what?"

Placing the calm child in the arms of a servant, he once again gripped her arm and dragged her from the room. Although he didn't hold her as tightly, his intent was the same. As they came closer to the door, she could hear the people screaming for her blood and began to struggle.

"You can't be serious! STOP! No! Don't do this Alcherist!" Throwing her weight back suddenly, he lost his grip on her and she fell. Trying to scramble away, he leaned over and grabbed a handful of her raven hair. "Help! Please! Someone help me!"

She knew no one would come to her aid, but she had to try. The Dark Lord had promised to rescue her. He would not abandon her now. She just needed a bit more time. She twisted her body and kicked him with all her might, nothing worked. He dragged her down the few steps and into the courtyard.

"HEAR ME!" Alcherist shouted to the soldiers holding the gate. "Bring me the leader of this mob!"

The captain of the guard reached through the gate speaking briefly and dragged someone inside. Gradually the crowd grew quiet, straining to hear what would happen.

"What's your name?" Alcherist asked the man, dragging Sybella up to stand, disheveled, at his side. The man gave a small bow and looked at Sybella as he answered, "I'm only a servant, My Lord. What would you have me do?"

Sybella stilled and looked at the man closely. Lowering her head, she used the curtain of hair to block the small smile on her face. So, this was the moment, the Dark Lord had sent Chumbra to rescue her.

"The mob has indicated you as its leader. Here!" He thrust Sybella into the man's grasp. "Take her and do what you will. She is no longer my concern." Alcherist turned and stormed back into his home to tend to his family. He would explain to Ashrek that he had been overrun and had no choice but to hand her over to the mob. The boy would get over the loss of his child, much in the same way they had told him to do regarding Khal.

"How do you plan to get us through this crowd?" Sybella whispered as the captain of the guard escorted them back to the gate.

"What crowd?" Chumbra asked.

Stepping through the gate, she saw only empty streets, but looking back at the top of the gate, she could see the soldiers yelling and threatening any who dared come close.

"An illusion my dear, the people of this town are weak minded but cowardly when it comes to an actual fight. It did not take much to cast a spell. Now hurry, the Dark Lord is waiting for us." He led her outside the city to where he had left two horses and they disappeared into the night.

Chapter 39

AKRONIUS STOOD ON THE FROZEN river bank; it had been two days since Alric crossed the river. Elainea refused to eat as she worried over him. Kaison trained daily with Naia and he had taken his first flight with Syphra. He had even transformed fully and although he was only able to hold that form for a breath, it was exhilarating and exhausting. He turned and headed back to the house. Keuri and her group had been training with them as well. Together they were strong but still needed more people.

Akronius watched silently as Keuri sparred with Elainea. The girl's red hair whipped around her head like a firestorm. She moved through the attacks with deadly precision and focus, it was like watching an intricate dance. She was no longer the girl he tracked through the mountains; she'd matured into a fierce lioness. She had traded her split skirts for leather pants and wore a leather vest over a wool shirt, all gifted to her from Keuri. It suited her.

"Keuri, can I speak to you a moment?" Akronius said, never taking his eyes off Elainea who smiled broadly at him through her sweat soaked face.

"Of course, but looking at me would help." She chuckled as Elainea walked toward the river. "She's a strong woman. You could do much worse."

"She is like a sister to me. I'm proud of who she has become, despite what she has gone through," Akronius said.

"Hmm, I suppose so. Where I'm from all the women are trained at a far younger age than she," Keuri noted. "But, she is strong. I pity the man who tries to control her."

"So do I!" Akronius laughed. "Now, we need more people to fight with us. With every villager scared for their lives or fleeing to Vimeo, recruiting is not working. Is there any chance that more southerners would be willing to follow you here?"

"Yes." Keuri said, taking a drink of water from the skin she kept nearby.

"Yes..?" Akronius asked with uncertainty.

Keuri drew her hand across her mouth and smiled. "When we came, we left a large group waiting for word of what we found here. We may not agree that Alric is strong enough to be king, but with the guidance of his father and you, he is a far cry better than David. I'll let them know to come quickly."

Closing her eyes, Keuri began to swirl her hand in an intricate pattern, causing a strong wind to rise around her. When it had reached a crescendo, she pushed it away to the south. "Done, they will be here as soon as they're able."

Akronius looked at her skeptically. "They will follow a breeze?"

Keuri laughed at the expression on his face. "It was a prearranged signal. My wind would mean we fight together. An earthquake would have been a refusal. Don't worry, they'll come."

Keuri walked off to rejoin her group and let them know of the decision as Akronius went to find Syphra. He could feel eyes following him and knew it was the wolves. They were as large as he had thought and twice as scary. He was glad they were on their side. As the first line of defense, they constantly patrolled the tree line, since the spy was caught, periodically checking in with Kaison or himself.

Just then, Kaison came jogging from the forest with Naia at his side, over his shoulder was slung the carcass of a deer.

"Akronius, any sign of Alric yet?" He asked as he hung the deer up for skinning.

"None." Akronius sighed. "If he doesn't return soon, we'll have to confront David without him."

"You know we can't do that. Alric has to be the one to do it and claim the throne."

"Are you sure about that? The prophecy is not exactly specific on the *who* part, and as much as you may want to deny it, Alric..." Akronius struggled for the right words to say without offending the boy's father. "Alric is... well... he's not exactly..."

"I know Akronius. I know." Kaison said sadly. "I can't help but wonder if he would be stronger if things had not turned out as they have. All we can do is push him to be who we need him to be, and hope for the best."

"You saw how he lashed out after harboring a small amount of resentment, even if he was under the power of that cursed stone. If we push him too much into something he doesn't want, it could have the opposite effect. We could lose him to the darkness completely.

134

Maybe…" Akronius looked Kaison in the eye. "Maybe you should consider taking the throne again. Only until you could train Alric as he needs, or until someone else could be adequately groomed."

Kaison said nothing, his gaze fixed on the now frozen river. Hesitantly, Akronius placed a hand on Kaison's shoulder. "All I ask is that you consider it. Right now, you're our best choice." He squeezed and let go, walking to the barn leaving Kaison alone with his thoughts.

Chapter 40

'DO YOU UNDERSTAND?'

"Yes, I do. I won't let you down." Alric said with a genuine smile.

'You could never be a disappointment Alric. You are exactly as you were meant to be and will do exactly what you were meant to do. Keep the faith. I love you.'

Those final three words felt like a gentle caress across his heart and embedded themselves in his soul. He watched the figure return to the tree and with one final soul-piercing gaze, disappear. Alric turned and headed back into the woods. He no longer feared the wolves or the darkness, even though he saw them slinking on the periphery of his vision. They neither advanced nor retreated. Turning to face the nearest one, he stopped, for every step toward it he took, the creature took one step back and growled. When Alric took another step forward, it whimpered and Alric smiled. No, he was not afraid, but they were. Maybe not of him, but of the light he now represented.

With the setting sun, the sky had turned to a bronze glow reflecting across the frozen river. Gazing to the other side, Alric saw Keuri and her group laughing around a fire. Elainea sat with them, but only gazed sadly into the flames, huddled beneath a large blanket. Alric focused on the flames and formed a small shield around one tongue, lifting it slowly. He watched everyone sit up in shock. Moving it toward his sister, he placed it in her outstretched hand.

"Alric…" Elainea whispered. Closing her hand around the flame, she quickly stood, "ALRIC!" She raced to the river just as he floated across and into her outstretched arms.

"Hi Laney." He whispered in her ear. He felt the tears of relief land on his shirt. "I'm alright now. Let's go see the others."

Keeping one arm around each other, they approached the silent camp. Akronius and Kaison had come to stand near the fire, a myriad of questions playing across their faces as their breath puffed in the frigid night air.

"I can't tell you everything that happened, only that I found what I needed. Akronius, can I see the sword please."

Akronius went and retrieved the sword and handed it over. "Are you sure you should be doing this?"

"Trust me." Alric said with a smile. Turning to his sister, "I need you to make a fire as hot as you possibly can," he said.

Elainea lifted her hands and the flames went from orange to red to blue and then white. Alric once again formed a small shield around the flame and then levitated the sword into the middle of it.

"Alric, Shama said the sword could not be destroyed, only the flames of Arcana can do that." Elainea said with concern.

"I'm not trying to destroy it," he answered, watching the sword glow and soften with the heat. "Only separating and repurposing it. Okay, pull the heat away."

Elainea called the flame back to herself as well as drawing the heat from the blade. Dropping to the ground, the red stone rolled off to the side and where it had sat in the pommel, a sun design replaced it, its rays etched and reaching up the blade intricately.

"How did you…" Kaison looked at his son who only shook his head slightly. "What happened in the wood?"

"Like I said, I can't tell you. What I can say is how hungry I am!"

"Of course, you are," Elainea laughed, tugging him toward the house. "Your father brought home a deer this morning. There is some stew left over."

Kaison and Akronius silently watched the two walk into the home. "He seems different, doesn't he?" Kaison asked.

"Yes, focused maybe. Determined. He held eye contact with me, where before, he was always quick to look away," Akronius said.

"Yes, and his control has increased as well. What he did to the sword…"

"If he can channel that control and focus it into fighting, we may stand a chance against David." Akronius said, clapping a hand on his comrade's shoulder.

"I'll work with him. He'll be ready." Kaison said with a firm nod. Alric was his son. He would make sure he was ready.

Chapter 41

ASHREK LAY IN HIS BED shivering and weak, this was that witch's fault, he just knew it. How she had managed to curse him, he did not know, but he would not let her win. Because of the purge, he did not have access to any of the dark arts she would have used to hurt him. But he was not foolish enough to think he had cleaned his land in such a short time. He had sent his men out the night before with instructions to go door to door until they found someone loyal to the Dark Lord, someone still practicing dark magic.

The door opened and the captain walked in dragging an old man with him. "We found one Sir."

"Good. Bring him closer." Just those few words and Ashrek felt winded, he did not know how much longer before all his strength was gone. "What do you know... about this... curse? How... can it... be... broken."

The old man looked at Ashrek and sneered. "I have no reason to help you. I hope you die!" Feeling proud of himself, he drew what he could from his throat and spit in Ashrek's face.

With no energy to even wipe it away, Ashrek looked at the guard and nodded slightly.

The man was dragged to the fireplace and his hand thrust into the flames. The smell of burning flesh filled the air and his agonized screams rang against the stone walls.

"I will ask... once more. And then... the guards... will do this... to anyone... left... in your home." His whispers sounded more menacing than if he had yelled.

"Ahh, Ahh, mmmmhmmm" the man whimpered, sitting on the floor clutching his charred hand to his chest. His eyes glazed over from the pain. "Check your body for scratches or punctures. Everywhere, look everywhere, look, look!" As his head started to loll to the side, the guard delivered a kick to his ribs that knocked him to his back on the floor.

"You'll die in two days without a cure...poultice to cut off flow of power, to the... the wearer of... the charmed item." The man's eyes rolled back into his head and though his chest continued to rise and fall, he said no more.

"Take him... away. Find... another."

"Yes, My Lord." The guard dragged the unconscious man down the hall to an abandoned room. He was hit with the scent of death and human waste as he opened the door and tossed the man inside. He stumbled backwards just as the door was closing, as if someone had pushed him out of the way. Looking up and down the hall he saw nothing. Sighing, he headed back to the village to find another victim for Lord Ashrek. The hair on the back of his neck continued to prickle as if someone watched him. The feeling did not vanish until he was outside the gates of the manor.

Chapter 42

AKRONIUS STOOD PROUDLY WATCHING ALRIC and Kaison spar. It had been several days since he returned and the change was evident. Gone was the boy who wielded a sword half-heartedly and saw his gifts as useless and weak. Alric attacked with strength, using the repurposed sword and blocked with a created blue shield on his opposite arm. Sweat dripped down his face, but he didn't complain as he once would have. His dark eyes were hard, despite the smirk he held, tracking the movement of his father.

Kaison didn't go easy on him, he refused to soften his attacks, the enemy wouldn't. They moved quickly, neither willing to concede or give ground. Amid a flurry of sword thrusts and parries they ended with a blade placed at each other's throat, laughing they lowered their weapons.

"Well done Alric! I am glad you took Akronius' training to heart," Kaison said, breathing rapidly.

"How could I not, when, he threatened to feed me to Syphra if I didn't!"

Syphra rolled her eyes as she watched from a short distance away. "She says you are too skinny to be more than a mouthful and not worth the trouble of picking your bones from her teeth." The other men turned to look at her and she snapped her teeth at them. Akronius laughed. Only he could hear the laughter in her voice.

"Speaking of mouthful, let's go eat." Alric said using a rag to wipe his face, he could not afford to let the cold bring sickness.

"You'll have to prepare your own meal. Your sister has been busy training with Keuri," Akronius said.

"It was brilliant to combine her fire with Keuri's wind. A flaming whirlwind will destroy anyone who is foolish enough to stand before them, and is a much appreciated source of heat!" Kaison agreed.

"Exactly, and the others will be threats as well. Sarta's lightning is terrifying up close." Akronius had been too close to her on multiple occasions. He was beginning to wonder if she did it on purpose to cause his hair to stand on end.

'Someone is traveling quickly on the trade road, two riders, one male and one female.'

"Kaison, there is…"

"I heard him." Kaison said in response to Nguvu's message to both of them. "People are running away from Elhaanai, not coming in. You should take Syphra and see who it is."

"No, she will be too easy to spot. I will find Nguvu," Akronius said sharply.

'Nguvu, where on the road are you?'

'Where the rotten tree fell.'

'I am on my way.'

Akronius hurried to meet Nguvu and determine who was coming into their territory, traveling as quickly and quietly as he could.

'Here. They have stopped to water their horses. I can smell the darkness in them. Do you know who they are?'

'Yes, that is Chumbra. Oracle to King David and follower of the Dark Lord. I'm not sure of the woman with him. Either she is a prisoner or a dark follower as well.'

'She is no prisoner, Akronius. He assisted her from the horse and they seemed at ease.' Placing his snout in the air, *'And she is carrying a child.'*

'Follow them as far as you can and report back to us.'

Akronius slipped back into the shadows and returned to the cottage to inform the others of Chumbra's activities.

"Chumbra, what is the hurry! You do see the condition I am in. I need to rest," Sybella moaned, as she stretched her back and walked toward some shrubbery near the river to relieve herself.

"Yes, yes. You're pregnant. Not only have you said it repeatedly, but I can clearly see your broad waistline! I don't know why the Dark Lord needs a whining woman like you, but he does and we need to hurry! Not everyone is loyal to our master. Rebels are hiding everywhere. I don't want to spend another night under these stars."

"And you say, I whine. Listen to your sniveling. It's no wonder the Dark Lord needs me, if he is surrounded by weaklings such as you. Now, help me back on the horse."

Doing as he was bid, the two continued toward King David,

completely unaware of the silent hunter stalking them.

Everyone gathered around Akronius as he relayed what he'd seen. "I don't know who the woman is, but she travels with Chumbra heading toward Nuru Manor! We can only assume she's not going there to kill him." He nodded to Keuri. "We have more help coming from the South in a few weeks. When they get here, we must be ready to either march against David or against Arcana. We'll be too large in number to stay here."

"Agreed! Alric, you have made tremendous progress in the last few days," Kaison said, placing a hand on his son's shoulder. "I'm proud of you and will be prouder still to follow you as my King."

"Thank you, Father. I am stronger, but with strength comes wisdom. The prophecy is only specific in saying that the dead king will return," nodding to his father, "and that there will be one death, who we assume, means David, and the evil of the Dark Lord filling something hollow."

Alric knew his next words would shatter everyone's beliefs, but it was his task to complete, drawing from the strength he'd gained at the foot of the great tree he continued. "I learned a lot while I was away. One of those things is the true words of the prophecy. Shama got one thing wrong, or maybe we needed to believe his version first and he intentionally left the last line out. I don't know. But the prophecy actually says,

'When the dead King returns, darkness will follow. Evil will fill places left hollow. One throne, one life, one death to claim, one to alter, one to change.. The One to judge the two between, no pawn, no rook, no bishop nor king."

Alric looked around and wondered how long it would take for them to come to the same conclusion he had. Meeting Akronius' eyes, he saw the understanding dawn in them as he turned to Elainea…

"That only leaves… the Queen."

The End

I really hope that you enjoy this story.

If you have a moment to leave me a review I would really appreciate it. Without reviews, it is very hard to grow a book's audience. Keep reading for a sneak peak at the final book in the Tales of Elhaanai Series, Wages of War.

With sincere thanks, Nicole

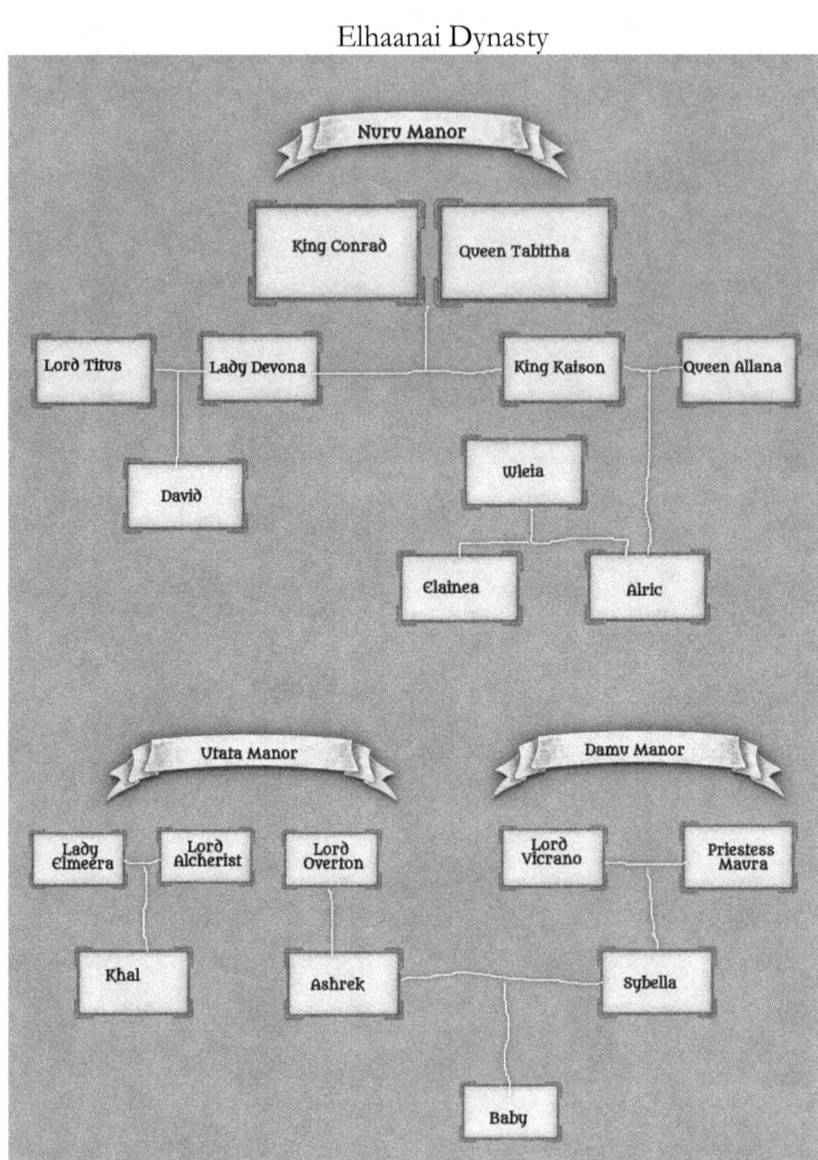

Nuru Manor
King Conrad
Queen Tabitha
Lord Titus
Lady Devona
King Kaison
Queen Allana
David
Wleia
Elainea
Alric
Utata Manor
Lady Elmeera
Lord Alcherist
Lord Overton
Khal
Ashrek
Damu Manor
Lord Vicrano
Priestess Mavra
Sybella
Baby

About The Author

Nicole Thomas was born in Queens, New York in 1984. She has been married for 10 years and has one daughter and one cat. For her "Outside of church, there is nowhere more refreshing for my soul than curled up in a corner with chocolate and a good book." And that love led into writing. She has always enjoyed reading, her favorite genres being Christian fiction, historical fiction and fantasy. Tales of Elhaanai, her first novel, is a mystical blending of those genres. Early one morning Nicole heard Alanna's voice as she ran for her life through the mists. That is how Elhaanai was born. She is currently working on the third book in The Elhaanai saga.

Follow along with me @NicolePatriceT on Twitter and IG.

Books in the Elhaanai Series

Tales of Elhaanai - Book 1

The desire for power is the root of all evil, betrayal is the currency to get it and keep it, by any means necessary. The one with the most strength and faith, be they good or evil, will be the victor. Join Alric and his friends as they walk the road to destiny.

The Prophecy- Book 2

They made it to the top of the mountain, only to return home and find heartbreaking waiting. Enemies have become allies and death does not always mean dead. Alric, Elainea and their small band of warriors take the next steps towards destiny and an outcome they may not be prepared for.

Other Books by this Author

Facets of A Poetic Soul

Within these pages are poems that describe moments in my life, moments in your life and moments in the life of someone you know. Emotions ranging from death to life, pain to joy and a bit of everything in between.

Acknowledgments

I would like to dedicate this book to my family, for continuously pushing me forward. To my nana, who shared my love of reading and believed in what she would not live to see. I miss you and I know you are proud of me. To my daughter, whose imagination never ceases to amaze me. To my husband, for never stopping me from talking about these books, I love you. To my Lord and Saviour, for the inspiration, direction and faith to see this through. To my readers, every single one of you is amazing and destined for greatness, if you allow the light to shine in and through you there will be no limit to your potential. Stay the Course.

Be Blessed.

Tales of Elhaanai
Wages of War

'When the dead King returns, darkness will follow. Evil will fill places left hollow. One throne, one life, one death to claim, one to alter, one to change. The One to judge the two between, no pawn, no rook, no bishop nor king.'

Alric looked around and wondered how long it would take for them to come to the same conclusion he had. Meeting Akronius' eyes, he saw the understanding dawn in them as he turned to Elainea…

"That only leaves…the Queen." Akronius whispered as all eyes turned to Elainea, whose tan skin turned an ashy grey.

"You can not be serious." She said, "You do not believe him right?" She looked around seeing the doubt and questions swirling across the faces of the others. It had been no secret that everyone had doubted Alrics' strength to be King, but surely they would not back him on this. It was madness and yet not one person spoke; she took a step back from the group shaking her head, "We have trained and practiced and people have DIED for you to be King. Our MOTHERS DIED believing you to be King, Alric!" She gazed deep into her brothers' grey eyes, pleading for him to recant and instead saw something she had never seen before and could not name, "I know you are afraid, but I will not allow you to hide behind that fear. You are meant to be King. I am not…I WILL not be Queen." Turning on her heels, Elainea quickly walked away from the group, away from her home, away from the pressure propelling her towards an unwanted future, towards the solitude of the forest.

Kaison started to go after her but Alric stopped him with a firm hand on his arm, "Let her go. She will understand in time. There is more I

148

need to tell you that she will not be prepared to hear right now." Casting one last worried glance towards the forest Kaison nodded and followed Alric as he sat by the fire, one by one the others in the group did the same.

"Will you tell us what happened to you in the wood?" Keuri asked

"No, I am sorry. That journey was meant only for me." Alric said with a smile, holding the small woman's gaze, "But what I learned is for all of us. The end of the prophecy is clear, as I have told you. And I do believe it means Elainea is meant to be Queen. It was no secret that you all tried to force yourselves to see me as King." Alric said it lightly so as not to offend anyone. Though his father looked guilty and Akronius would not meet his eye, "It is alright, I am meant to do great things, but being a King is not one of them. I will return to Shama once the war is over, and take his place on the mountain."

"What? What do you mean?" Kaison said in shock, "You may have the gift of sight but you are no oracle! How can you...why would you...no. You must be mistaken."

"Father, I know this will be hard to accept. I did not understand it at first either, but in time it began to make sense. Being an oracle is not necessary to be the guardian of the pool, only the ability to commune with The One. I can, I have and I will continue to do so until He says my work is done."

The fire crackled and a log split sending sparks flying as each person contemplated his words, "I'll admit, I did not hide my doubt in you when we first met", Keuri said, raising her green eyes from the dancing flames to meet his, "but we also believe David is not meant to be on the throne, you would only have been an improvement, albeit a weak one. With your fathers and Akronius' guidance, you would have made a fine King. But I will not fight you on this, none of us will." She said gesturing to her companions who nodded in agreement

"Thank you Keuri." Alric smiled, "I apologize for holding you as I did on our first meeting. You are a strong woman and a strong ally. Elainea will need people like you around her." Keuri dipped her head once in acknowledgement. "Father, Akronius, this is the way it must be. The One has confirmed it to me and I need you to trust me as I trust Him."

"Alric," Kaison scrubbed his hand over his face, gathering his thoughts, "Son, I know you think this is what must be but, how can it? She is not of noble birth. She has no experience or training in ruling. She is part of your family and this group but no one outside of this home even knows who she is. There has never been a Queen on the throne of Elhaanai. I am sorry, I must disagree with you on this."

"I agree with him, Alric." Akronius said solemnly, "Elainea is a strong woman but she is no queen. This makes no sense."

Looking at both men Alic smiled, "And who am I? I have had no ruling experience or training. If not for you being alive, no one would be able to say if I were of noble birth or not because I was NOT of noble birth. To any who know me, Wleia was my mother. Our mother. I know it is hard to believe, but you will see in time."

Silence settled over the group as Alrics' words sank in, the truth in them undeniable. The flames crackled and smoke wafted into sky, floating to the heavens along with the doubts and questions on everyone's mind.

Elainea paced back and forth just beyond the tree line, she felt the wolves watching from the shadows, guarding but distant. The air around her rippled in the heat radiating from her skin, her anxiety forcing her to release partial control of her gift. *They are wrong. There is absolutely no WAY this is the path my life is meant to take. Alric is King, he will be King.* The thoughts twisted around and around in her head and her breathing became more and more erratic. She could feel the pressure rising as angry tears tracked down her face and her shoulders and chest heaved with each breath. She felt betrayed for some reason, misled and lied to. She was supposed to see Alric to the throne and then go on with her life, marriage to a good man, children, her own home. She had never voiced those desires but believed they would all come true in time. All of that had potentially been stripped away from her with a few words from Alric. No! She had given up the past few years for him, she did not resent him for it but she would not also relinquish her future to rule an entire kingdom.

The fire burned and pulsed just beneath the surface of her skin, causing her whole body to glow slightly red. She had never been this out of control before, she needed a release and quickly. Walking further into the forest and parallel to the river she came to a small outcropping of boulders. Planting her feet firmly and facing the largest of the rocks she raised her hands and almost threw the fire out. A steady stream of flames emerged from her palms and surrounded the boulders like a raging river but it wasn't enough; her tears created a fine haze around her face, evaporating before they could fall from her eyes. Thoughts of the life she would not have, the responsibility she would continue to have to shoulder, the potential addition of a kingdom brought her to her knees. She had always been the stable one, the mature and calm one, but not now. Now she screamed and opened every part of herself to the fire, she did not care about the trees around her or the stones or any animals caught in her blaze, for the first time she only cared about herself and the release, the letting go.

Coming May 2021

151

www.ingramcontent.com/pod-product-compliance
Lightning Source LLC
Chambersburg PA
CBHW070657100726
47907CB00007B/2243